A NICE GAZEBO

A Nice Gazebo

R O B Y N   S A R A H

Véhicule Press

"The Pond, Phase One," "Heading into Winter," and "New Management," first appeared in *Canadian Fiction Magazine*. "Furniture" appeared in *Queen's Quarterly*, "A Minor Incident" in *Canadian Author &Bookman*, and "Première Arabesque" in *Rubicon*.

Ludwig Wittgenstein's *Tractatus Logico-Philosophicus*, quoted in the story "Heading into Winter," is published by Routledge & Kegan Paul Ltd. (London, 1961).

Published with the assistance of The Canada Council.

Fiction series editor: Linda Leith
Cover photo: Mark Garland
Cover photo treatment and design: J.W. Stewart
Design and imaging: ECW Type & Art
Printing: Imprimerie d'Édition Marquis Ltée

CANADIAN CATALOGUING IN PUBLICATION DATA

Sarah, Robyn, 1949–
  A nice gazebo

ISBN 1-55065-034-3

  I. Title

PS8587.A3765N43 1992   C813'.54   C92-090425-4
PR9199.3.S27N43 1992
  79064

Véhicule Press, P.O.B. 125, Place du Parc Station, Montreal, Quebec H2W 2M9.
Distributed in Canada by General Distribution Services, and in the United States by Inland Book Company (East Haven, CT) and Bookslinger Inc. (St. Paul, MN).

Printed in Canada on acid-free paper.

CONTENTS

For my mother,
whose gift of a "Huge 10¢ Scribbler"
one day in 1956 started all this.

The Pond, Phase One

WHAT DO HUSBANDS, sitting on the front porch in the dark, talk about while their wives take a late night walk down a country road? One at a time, they rise abruptly and go into the house to freshen their drinks; they return, ice cubes clinking in their glasses, and settle down to take their ease; the dark beyond the edge of the deck is alive with lightning-bugs. A match flares, then another, and blue smoke of Sobranie wafts from one's pipe; the other's cigarette is a point of orange tracing the movement of his hand as he gestures across the valley, at house lights perhaps, to say who lives there, or maybe he's really indicating something nearer, the place they've bulldozed recently for a pond, not visible in the dark; he describes it to his guest.

I believe that for long periods they are silent, either because they do not feel the need to talk or because they think there is nothing very much to say; they're past that, they think, they're not young men any more. Probably when a child begins to wail in the bedroom upstairs where all three have been put to sleep, it doesn't register right away, it goes on for a little while before they remember that the women are not in the house. They think of it as the same moment and incline their heads — "Is that one of mine?"

"No, I think it's mine," and the host gets up and goes inside to check.

Their wives have been friends for upwards of twelve years; they met working in the same department for one of the larger weeklies in the city. Helen writes for a different paper now; Rosalie has been living in the country for two years, freelancing in her spare time, rueful to report she doesn't have the kind of spare time she expected to have. They miss their frequent long lunches together in the city, the telephone conversations that left receivers warm in their cradles in both houses — conversations comparing notes on everything from writing assignments to pediatricians and daycares to past loves, with long vivid digressions about their childhoods. They've seen each other through divorce, remarriage, pregnancy, childbirth, miscarriage and family illness; there is nothing they're afraid to say to each other. And now they find themselves the mothers of three children born within two years of each other, children who play together like cousins.

It has taken Rosalie two years in the country to be able to walk out at night without being driven back by a primitive dread of the dark — even on a night like this, starry, with a clear half-moon, and all the lightning-bugs twinkling on either side of the road. But Helen feels she could walk forever; she's utterly at home, she feels embraced by this country dark. Why? In the city, night gives her the creeps, even in her own neighbourhood. Here it's as if she could come to no harm; she imagines walking alone, breathing the fragrant air, following a road without knowing or caring where it may take her, just walking on and on into daybreak. She longs to do it. She feels immune, protected. Her husband, on the other hand, she tells Rosalie, gets spooked in the country at night. Once they took a walk down a road in Vermont, it was so beautiful, their first time in the country in years, and then he wanted to go back. Because there was that kind of a moon, a smoky moon, smothered in cloud. Rosalie says she knows exactly what kind of a moon. She gets spooked too.

They're quiet for a little while, then they begin making plans for the next day, for the three days Helen and Tom and the children can stay this time, before they have to go back to the city. It'll be wonderful next summer, when the pond has filled up. Is that all it takes? Helen wants to know; will one year's melting snow really make a pond? No, says Rosalie, but the hole is full of springs. You'll see tomorrow, we dug there because it was always marshy, and it turned out there are four or five underground springs. Right now it's just a big hole in the ground, with a hard mud bottom. But it's funny — Benjamin has been spending whole days down there playing, it's such a boon I almost wish we could leave it a mud-hole!

Little by little their talk moves to other things, the things they've been waiting to talk about, now they're over the first rise and far enough down the road that they can be sure their voices won't carry back toward the house. They speak fondly and ruefully of the state of their marriages, tentatively of the men they are currently in love with: in Rosalie's case her first cousin, a painter, recently divorced and living in the next township, in Helen's a colleague, also married, with whom she used to car-pool — a man lately fired for political reasons, and in the process of filing a grievance.

They tell of recent exchanges, they are amazed at the parallels; they laugh at themselves. It's a relief to be able to talk about it. What's the matter with us? It's so stupid. Do you think it's the same for everyone? Helen has a friend who's in love with a priest; Rosalie says so-and-so told her she and her husband haven't slept together for four months and she's in love with a doctor at the hospital where she works. God, says Helen, four months, that's even worse than us. And a doctor. Couldn't she do better than that? They laugh because it's a long-standing joke between them, their indifference to the professional set, their preference for the crazy ones, artists, politicos, dreamers — the ones they left the first time around.

The damp gravel crunches under their sandals. Rosalie yawns. Do you think we should turn back now? Maybe we'd better. They might worry. Do you suppose the kids ever settled down? They were so excited to see each other. Funny how light it seems now, I can see everything. I'm getting eaten alive by mosquitoes, what about you?

2

The hole has been dug right to hardpan, with banks that slope, though it's to be expected that the sides will give somewhat when the pond fills up. At the bottom the mud is mostly firm, traced by rivulets from the springs. The water is icy cold and good to drink; one of the springs bubbles up from under a rock, you can catch the water in your hands. Any quick spots? Tom wants to know. A few, Daniel says, but nothing dangerous to the children — the hole's too deep for that. They could sink in maybe half a foot, probably not even that.

Nevertheless Amy, the youngest, loses no time in finding one; before breakfast eggs have even hit the pan the boys come running, banging the screen-door, Mummy, Daddy, Amy's stuck in the mud and she can't get out!

Ludicrous in her nightgown and Wellingtons, Helen runs out after them into morning mist, down into the raw gash in the landscape behind the house. She feels her own foot give as she steps out onto the flat where Amy, arms upraised and wailing, stands with mud nearly to the tops of both red gum-boots. Backing up, she tests for solid footing and leans over to get her hands under Amy's arms. The suck of the mud is surprisingly strong; twice she loses her balance, and in the end lifts Amy clear minus one boot, and has to go back for it.

She recognizes that there's no real danger, Tom and Daniel josh her out of that, but after breakfast, when the children indicate they're heading back down there, she wants to go too, to see for herself just how much trouble Amy is apt to get into if left on her own there. Rosalie says she'll come too, she likes the mud-hole. It's not the way you'd think, she says, it's really kind of an interesting thing to have in one's back yard. I feel like it wouldn't be a complete disaster if it *didn't* fill up.

The children troop ahead, jubilant explorers; the women, skirts catching in the tops of their Wellingtons, pick their way down along the tracks the bulldozer left on its way out. They'll come back in the fall, Rosalie explains, to bank up the far side where the springs drain off; the idea is to give the sides some time to harden.

At the bottom of the hole, an expanse of gleaming wet mud, variously textured. The silts are red and brown and grey and black, streamlets of water have deposited traces and superimposed them to create a marbling effect. Where springs bubble up, the silt is held in suspension; small fountains, small eddies of velvety mud. Mostly, it's surprisingly firm to walk on, but there are those spots near the springs where sediment has built up; when you step on them the mud gives, you sink rapidly, a little sickeningly, but not very far: to half the depth of her own boots, Helen discovers; Amy was about as far in as she could have gone. She finds it's hard, but not very, to extricate herself unaided, even without leaving a boot behind.

She tells Amy and Jeremy to stay away from the squishy parts. The only danger, agreed, is that they could lose their balance and tumble: more nuisance than danger. After all, we have a washing-machine, says Rosalie.

They follow behind the children, who are exploring the run-off, where rivulets merge into a shallow stream that wanders away crookedly among cattails toward the lower meadow. This is the part that will be blocked off in the fall. There will still be drainage, through a pipe, but not the same amount of water — only the overflow from the pond. You

see what I mean, Rosalie says, it's a fabulous place for them
to play. There's all that mud for a stomping-ground, and
then a whole stream to follow out of it. Frogs. Pretty
pebbles. A whole forest of cattails to hide in. And I can let
Ben play by himself down here. Once the pond fills up, I'll
always worry a little. Yes, it's wonderful, agrees Helen. They
stand side by side in the deepest part of the stream, watch-
ing the water trickle over the toes of their boots, bending
to pick up the occasional rock glinting wet in the sun. At a
distance now, the children's heads bob in and out among the
cattails. A cicada, the first of the day, hones his drill some-
where above them.

3

Kyona. I've never heard of it. It's a Japanese green, says
Rosalie. Taste it. I ordered the seeds from our catalogue.
Helen breaks off a feathery, antler-shaped leaf. Mmmmm.
It tastes a bit like Chinese lettuce. What a beautiful name,
Kyona. You could name a child that. You could, says Rosalie,
only it probably means lettuce-like, or something, in
Japanese.

They're squatting side by side in the garden, pulling
leaves into a colander for a dinner salad. What else will you
need for the quiche? Rosalie wants to know. Helen, nibbling
another leaf of kyona, considers. You can put almost any-
thing in it. Zucchini and carrots will be fine. Maybe some
chard. Some fresh parsley, if you have any. Tons, says Rosalie,

over there at the end of the herb plot, behind the chives. See the chives? The purple puff-balls. Aren't they huge, says Helen. They must be strong enough to get up and walk.

What else goes with quiche? Oh, says Helen, you don't have to make anything. Please. A big salad will be fine. Let me do it, I want to. All right, says Rosalie, then I'll do a lasagna tomorrow. I have a marvellous recipe. Did I show you the book last time you came out? The one from that restaurant in Ithaca? Everything in it is fabulous. There's a vegetarian chili, it uses bulgur instead of meat. Really? I'd like to try that. Sure, I'll show it to you later, you can write it down.

Absently they are chewing on raw green beans, snow peas, breaking them off the vines as they move along the rows. It feels funny, Helen says. What does? To be talking about recipes. Are we that far gone? They laugh. I know what you mean.

They're thinking about when they first met, about foreign films, political demonstrations. About all-night pizza joints, rooms without furniture, dinners on the floor. They sit back on their heels and gaze up at the house, nestled among trees, the soaring timbers of the new addition still raw, blond in the sun. When did it become necessary, Rosalie wonders, this elaborate shell, this extension of self?

A perfect zucchini, glossy, deep green, not too fat yet, with the furled drying blossom still stuck to its end. Feel it, don't they feel strange when you first pick them? Almost prickly. Oh, I know, says Rosalie, it's a riot, do you know Benjamin won't touch them? He can't stand the feeling, it drives him completely wild. Even green beans. I can't get him to pick green beans for me, he says they're hairy. Green beans! Helen exclaims. But it's hardly noticeable on green beans! It is to him, I can understand it, I'm sort of the same, says Rosalie. When I was a kid I wouldn't go near peaches. I think I was 22 before I could touch a peach without climbing walls. I mean, I still don't *buy* them, but if someone gives me one . . . Well, I find that mildly amazing, says Helen. What is it, an allergy? Not of the usual sort, says Rosalie. I wonder if there's a name for it? Yes, says Rosalie, I think they call it texture.

4

Benjamin, Jeremy, red head, dark head, over the garden fence. Benjamin's a year younger but nearly a head taller. Jeremy's gap-toothed, radiant through sweat and mud. They've taken their shirts off, mud streaks their torsos. Where's Amy? Why did you leave her by herself?

Mummy, the backs of my shorts is soaking. Mummy, there's water in my boot. We're making mud things, Mummy. Come and see. They're drying on a rock. Mummy, we like the squishy parts. We won't get stuck. We can just take our boots off. Can we take off our boots, Mummy? Amy already has hers off. The best mud for making things is the squishy parts. Can you come and see? Please?

Go, says Rosalie, I'll put these things in the fridge and come down in a few minutes. Is there anything we need from town? Swiss cheese. Right. I'll tell Daniel, he has to drive in for some plumbing parts.

There's a downward-sloping shelf of rock, large enough for both of them to sit on, embedded in the east bank of what will be the pond. They tuck their skirts in around them, brace their heels to keep from sliding and hug their knees. The afternoon heat is intense. Slowly Helen slips her feet, one at a time, out of her boots; she peels her socks off and wads them and stuffs them inside, flexes her toes into the breeze. Good idea, says Rosalie. The children, already freed of boots, are almost knee deep in one of the quick spots, stomping and squelching gleefully. Chanting something. How can they stand to do that *barefoot*?

Like monks stomping on grapes, says Rosalie. No, says Helen, they're softening it up to make a trap for monsters. They told me.

They've made mud meatballs and mud potatoes and mud sausages, misshapen blobs drying in a row in a groove of the rock. Here come more. We'll show you how we make them, Mum. See this mud? See how you squish the water out? That's a very nice mudball, dear, but please get it away from my skirt. Squish the water out over there. Not in my hair. Mummy, you're knocking our dry potatoes down the hill. Look, Mum, it rolled right down and it didn't break! Look, Benjamin! Mine didn't break. Let's see if yours does. Let's see whose breaks. Amy, come! We're playing Potato Rolling Down The Hill!

Tom and Daniel have driven to town, Rosalie says, they may drive around a bit before coming back. They promised to be back in time for supper. There's a garage sale on in Dunsmuir they might check out, we're looking for bicycles. Benjamin, I like your mudball very much but I told you to take it over there. No, *further*. Where it won't drip on me.

Here, Mummy, hold this, I have to get some more of the wet stuff. Jeremy, I don't *want* to hold it. Put it down. Anywhere. Ouch, don't *lean* on me, honey, it's hard to keep my balance on this rock — Rosalie, will you listen to us, Helen laughs suddenly, you'd think we'd never read *Summer-hill*. Really — just like a couple of *mothers*, sitting primly on our nice dry rock. Aren't you afraid we're going to stifle their creative spirit?

A whoop from Rosalie. I know, aren't we awful? They don't look very stifled to me. I suppose if we were really enlightened, we'd sit down in the mud and make potatoes with them. She waves a deerfly away from her head. Well, so there you are, says Rosalie, suddenly serious, the career, the kid, the countryhouse. Everything I always said I wanted. You'd think I could sit back now and enjoy it all.

Can't you? asks Helen. Why can't you? She shifts her position on the rock; another potato rolls down the slope. I don't know, says Rosalie, I'm consumed with restlessness. She picks up one of the smaller dried mudballs and presses it between thumb and forefinger to see how hard it is. It explodes softly, showering damp sand in her lap; she brushes it off her skirt.

I am too, says Helen. Ever since the kids stopped being babies. Give me one of those. They're sort of neat, aren't they? It cracks between fingers like a soft nut, slightly off-centre; the two halves, each intact, lie in her palm. One of them has a small pebble imbedded in it; that's what it cracked around.

What do you think, asks Rosalie, would you have an affair with Peter? Helen is leaning over the edge of the rock, scooping some of the wet mud into her palm. She spreads it carefully with a finger, picking out all the tiny pebbles, every little irregularity. I don't know, she says slowly. It hasn't exactly come up. There's a lot at stake for both of us, we don't seek each other out. When I see him it's nice, is all.

She's squeezing the mud in her fist, it molds to her hands, holding the ridges where it pressed between her fingers. She reshapes it into a ball, more perfectly formed than the ones the children have made, and sets it in the groove to dry. There must be a lot of clay in this. It has a wonderful texture. Has it? says Rosalie. They both lean over, digging with their fingers for handfuls.

I think about Martin all the time, says Rosalie. I even think about having another kid just to get him off my mind. And then I think — well, *no*. You're right, there must be a lot of clay in this. It feels almost alive. No wonder the kids are so enthralled.

They discover that tossing the mud from hand to hand is a good way to get the excess water out. At first it has a slick wet slap to it; it's elastic, the momentum pulls it into odd loose shapes in the air. But as it gets drier, it firms up, it packs into a smooth dense ball, a small planet, you can squeeze it and it will keep its form. Suppose we baked these, says Helen, would they harden like clay does? Let's keep a few and try, says Rosalie. Let's make a few specially, with the smoothest mud we can find.

They leave the rock and wade across the web of little streams, holding up their skirts. The mud is sun-warmed now, smooth as skin, and near the source of the main spring there's a part that seems to breathe beneath them; they feel it give a little and surge back with every step, retaining its surface tension. It's like walking on somebody's stomach, says Rosalie. Isn't it? says Helen. You can see why this is the stuff God is supposed to have made Adam out of.

5

The children's voices are far away down the stream, they've evolved out of the mud, moved on to other things. Here and there you can see the print of a small foot that sank in sideways; the quick spots are all churned up, they're a lighter colour than the rest. Helen and Rosalie are squatting by one, they've tucked the bottoms of their skirts up into their waistbands; their hands, their wrists, their forearms are plunged deep in mud. There's something hypnotic about it, they aren't even making mudballs any more.

They look at each other suddenly and begin to giggle. What is this, play therapy? I don't know, but it sure is fun. How long have we been down here, anyway? You've got some in your hair. Well, you've got some on your forehead. What are we going to tell the guys when they ask what kept us from starting dinner earlier? If we don't get up to the house soon and wash, says Rosalie, we won't have to tell them anything.

Oh, who cares what they think! says Helen. I haven't had so much fun in ages. Can you believe it? A whole afternoon! Hey, says Rosalie, look over there, the kids have come back around by the field. They're over by the rock. Hey, don't touch those, she yells. Those are *our* mudballs. Leave them alone, we want to bake them!

Don't touch our mudballs! they yell, and then they're collapsing, gasping, holding their stomachs, their hands are so mucky they can't even wipe their streaming eyes. Rosalie, says Helen, when she can talk again, as long as we've regressed this far, why not take off our clothes and get right in? I mean, they're going to think we're crazy anyway. Can you imagine? What on earth would they make of it?

You just reminded me, says Rosalie, that when I was in college, in the dorm, I used to fantasize about taking a bath in chocolate pudding. I even got as far as measuring the tub and figuring out how many packages it would take.

You did? Honest? How many packages *was* it? Helen sounds amazed, subdued. Did you ever do it? No, says Rosalie sadly, it was too expensive.

They're clutching themselves again, they're doubled over, when they finally straighten up it's as if something has gone out of them, they're limp, drained; they feel wobbly and innocent as newborn colts.

Well? says Helen.

I will if you will.

I will if you will.

They untie their cotton wrap-around skirts, they slip out of their nylon bikini-briefs, they throw off their halter-tops and fling them up the bank toward the rock. Flimsy summer fabrics, ballooning, bright, arc upward to tumble in a heap. Breasts bouncing, they splash across the stream to the deepest quick-spot; solemnly, dispassionately, they watch their feet disappear; with whoops, they fall to their knees in velvet bubbling mud.

The hum of a car engine, just become audible in the distance, will be Tom and Daniel. They've got two used ten-speeds roped through the windows to the roof of the car, and they're taking it slow and easy over the hill.

Heading into Winter

SHE LEFT THE CAT. She intended at first (or so she said) to come back for it, it was always more her cat than his, though they'd had it together from a kitten when they'd first shared rooms. She did come back, once she found an apartment to her liking, after a few months of "camping out" with various friends, renting rooms and moving out of them because they didn't suit her, and visiting her mother and sister in California. She came back to pack up the rest of her books and to arrange about moving the piano, but she didn't take the cat. Her roommate was allergic, she said, and anyway, he'd had the cat alone all this time and probably it would be happier staying with him. If he didn't mind.

The truth was, he had gotten quite attached to the cat since she'd left, and he'd been planning to give her a hard time about taking it, but the flippancy with which she now consigned it to him was galling, so he only shrugged. He stood with his hands in his pockets and watched her pile paperback books and sheet music into a battered foot-locker which she said her brother would come for with the car tomorrow night. Would he be home tomorrow night? If not, could he leave her a key? He told her he would be home. He rolled himself a cigarette and offered to roll her one, but she said No, thanks, Michael, and flashed him a peculiarly pained look, apologetic or affronted or both, he couldn't tell, probably neither, probably he was reading into it, maybe she quit smoking. He wondered who her room-mate was. She'd had her hair cut very short, it came to a sort of point at the nape of her neck and he found himself staring at this as she bent over the piles of books on the floor. She had a long, graceful neck and the fact that she wore no jewellery made it seem longer. She was deeply tanned.

The cat, which had greeted her with no more display of affection than if she'd been gone a day, sat hunched on top of the piano, purring faintly, with half-shut eyes. Its tail banged lazily against the base of the lamp it sunned itself under. Its expression, seeming to belie the purr, was baleful. When she closed the foot-locker, it jumped down, striking a jarring chord in the bass en route to the floor, and rubbed against her legs.

"Oh, kitty." She picked it up for a moment and pressed her forehead against the flat of its head. "So long, kitty." And giving it a quick squeeze, she dropped it to the floor again, where it immediately resumed its hunch. They used to joke that it was part vulture.

"Well, Michael."

"Well," he said.

"I hope you've been doing okay?" she asked, hesitating, almost flustered. "I mean . . ."

"Oh, sure. I watch a lot of television." He meant to toss that off lightly, but he was aware as he said it that it sounded morose.

Again that look from her. "Well, if there's anything . . . I mean . . ." Suddenly she stepped towards him, catching him awkwardly off balance, and kissed him half on the cheek, half on the mouth. "Well, be seeing you, I guess."

"Yes," he said, and walked her to the door. He went out on the landing and watched her run down the stairs, not a run really, more of a springy walk, the soles of her sandals slapping back against her heels. The door at the bottom stuck; he heard it rattle as she tugged at the doorknob, then the Pock! of it opening and the clash when it banged behind her. A gust of cool air, September air, came up the stairs.

So long, Janet.

The cat, a female, had been one of a pair of kittens named Mason and Hamlin, after the piano. Mason succumbed early to the feline distemper. Hamlin, a calico, grew into a round and compact animal, harlequin, with the luxuriant tail of a Persian, though the rest of her fur was short. He called her Ham, Hammer, or Piggy, as befitted his whim and her humour. Her eyes were true green, not the yellow-green of most cats; the shade was not unlike Janet's, and, also like Janet, she had a way of looking right past you that suggested the visionary. She was not an affectionate animal; she had tolerated petting (from Janet only) with undisguised impatience, and she accepted all other attentions, whether in the form of food or invitations to play, as if they were no more than her due. She was, however, very nice to look at; and she had presence. She filled the place with it. Hamlin chased a ball of foil or cellophane, batting it around on the bare wooden floor with a lightning-white paw, deftly fishing it out from under furniture. Hamlin in her crouch on the kitchen table, front paws tucked demurely under her ruff, making piggy eyes at Michael's plate. Hamlin erect at the window, the razor edges of her ears flicking a radar for passing birds.

It wasn't true that he watched a lot of television, television bored him, but he had taken to leaving it on most of the day, with the sound tuned out, because Hamlin liked to lie on top of it when it got warm. Sometimes she would drape herself over the edge and peer at the screen, batting briefly at the image with her paw, but usually she just stretched full length on one side, tail thumping randomly, and stared into space with her wonderful round eyes. Michael would sink deep into the armchair kitty-corner and watch her; over the top of the jumping screen, for hours it seemed, they watched each other. He had the idea he might learn something this way. Mostly, in the end, he'd fall asleep.

Janet was the one who had liked to watch T.V. — "teevee" she called it, with a cozy intonation residual of a south Ontario childhood, ingenuous, like the way she had of sitting with her legs wide apart, the folds of a long, faded cotton skirt hanging between her knees. She made a little celebration of watching teevee, they'd watch the late-late movie together in bed, with mugs of hot cocoa and a big bowl of popcorn between them. She didn't care what was playing. If it was a horror picture he'd beg off and go into the other room to work on his dissertation, pretending disgust, though the embarrassing truth was that horror pictures scared him too much; even the music, coming through the wall, unnerved him at his labours. He always got a recap, anyway, from Janet when he turned in for the night, a garbled narrative spilling over itself with revisions and contradictions, punctuated by bursts of throaty laughter. She had the gift of not taking things too seriously.

And that, he supposed, was really why things turned out the way they had: he took things seriously. He took Janet seriously. At the beginning, her music, the hours of thundering Beethoven and Brahms, him having to go to the library to work, because the pianos at the Faculty were the pits, she said, never in tune, and most of them Yamahas, she hated Yamahas because they were tinny, only good for Hindemith and Webern, and she hated Hindemith and Webern too. And later, he took seriously her crisis of identity, realization she wasn't really concert material, resentment at the way she'd been pushed, as a child, so her focus was always music and there'd been no chance to explore, to find out who she was and what she wanted from life. It was his course, she told him then, the Introduction to Philosophy she'd taken as her academic option, that had really started her thinking about all that. Though it wasn't until after it was over that the shy girl from the Music Faculty, who sat in the back row far corner drawing pictures of sad-eyed women in the margins of her notebooks, knocked on the door of his office cubbyhole and came in to ask him if he really, um, you know, *believed* in a thing like a Categorical Imperative or an absolute system of ethics; wasn't it all culturally determined? It was 1970 and they were living together three weeks later; that, he supposed, was his answer.

He took seriously her depression after she withdrew from the Music Faculty, her brief involvements with therapy and meditation, her outbursts of rage at him for getting so wrapped up in his dissertation that he might as well be on the moon, her accusations that he flirted with his students. At the end, when she rarely got out of bed before four in the afternoon and then sat glowering in the armchair, chain-smoking, he took her silence seriously; he didn't intrude on it. And when she told him she had to get a place of her own, he assumed she knew what she needed. "If you're going to be lonely, you might as well be alone," that was how she put it. He wasn't sure whether she meant herself or him, but it didn't much matter. Maybe at that point he should have stopped taking her seriously. Yes, at that point he should have got mad and told her it was a bunch of horseshit. They should have had a good fight, banged up the furniture a bit and then laughed at each other, and made it up in bed, and stayed up all night watching teevee and stuffing their faces with popcorn.

Instead, here he was with a bogged-down dissertation on Wittgenstein, a warning from the chairman that if he wasn't able to wrap it up this year he stood to lose his teaching assistantship, and a cat. If you're going to be lonely, you might as well be alone. But he had Hamlin. There was that.

There was that, and there was Marnie from downstairs who knocked on his door once or twice a week and came in for tea and asked searching questions that he answered as evasively as possible; and there were a couple of his students that he went drinking with when he felt like it. There was Wittgenstein, but less and less of him. There was, in theory, the west coast, and there was Mexico, and there was learning to work with your hands. There was never exactly a conscious decision to scrap it all, but gradually, through the rainy weeks of fall, things seemed to conspire to point that way.

Things started to fall away. It began with the piano, hoisted out by three tattooed hulks armed with leather straps, leaving behind a neat fringe of dust along the floor and a collection of Hamlin's foil balls, like some bizarre clutch of eggs in the corner. The space thus suddenly freed gave him the idea of changing the furniture around, which led to his getting rid of a few other things — the monstrosity of an office desk that he'd sweet-talked Buildings and Grounds into giving him for Janet, and that she'd never used; the Victorian sofa whose arms Hamlin had scratched to threads.

Then, early in October, the apartment was broken into. The television and stereo were taken, and his portable typewriter (but there was still the old clunker in his office), and the 12-string guitar Janet had given him and he'd never learned to play. Hamlin was gone too. He got the janitor's permission to search the rabbit-warren of a basement, but had to conclude she'd gotten outside; two days of combing the alleys didn't turn her up. Janet and he had stopped letting her out at least a year before, but in the hope that she might still remember the way up by the fire-escape, he left the bedroom window open and shivered at night. On the third day he came back from school to find her stretched out regally on the bed. Her paws and ruff were grey, her fur damply greasy, and her tail matted and full of burrs. For removing which, his thanks was a long, deep scratch the length of his right forearm.

The fumigators were next. Somebody in the building, it seemed, had complained about the roaches and threatened to call the health department. At eight o'clock one morning, he was wakened by a volley of knocking, and stumbled to the door in his bathrobe to find a cadaverous Greek who informed him that he was to remove everything from his closets and kitchen cupboards, seal it all in big green plastic bags, leave them in the middle of the floor, and plan to be out for four hours the following afternoon, beginning at 1:30. It worked out fine because he had a three-hour lecture beginning at 2:00 and would have been out anyway. He tricked Hamlin into her Kitty Carrier and left her locked in his office.

When they returned, at dinnertime, the fumes were still overwhelming. Maybe that was what made putting all his things away seem an insupportable task. He opened a couple of bags and salvaged whatever he thought he really couldn't do without. Grocery staples, a couple each of dishes and utensils, a minimal cooking outfit, shaving gear, clothing that would fit in a hiker's pack. Then he re-sealed the bags, carried the lot of them down the fire-escape and around to the delivery entrance for the building, and made a note to call Salvation Army Pick-Up in the morning. Things, material objects, had begun to seem increasingly a drain on his energy. It felt good to divest himself of them.

Hamlin, after emptying her food dish and licking his, vomited on his bedspread. He guessed it was the fumes.

Language disguises thought. So much so, that from the outward form of the clothing it is impossible to infer the form of the thought beneath it, because the outward form of the clothing is not designed to reveal the form of the body, but for entirely different purposes.

A thought is a proposition with a sense.

The totality of propositions is language.

There was a time when I actually thought I understood this. When I thought I had something to say about it. Now I'm banging my head against even the first proposition. The world is all that is the case. *What case?*

He'd had the idea of beginning anew by copying out the whole of the *Tractatus Logico-Philosophicus* in longhand, on sheets of yellow newsprint. For a time it seemed to help. At least, it gave him the feeling that he was working; it assuaged his conscience. When he finished, he could start over, backwards, on rolls of paper towelling. (But do you get it? No, not really. L. W. wrote the thing in the trenches. In the fucking trenches! Maybe what I should really do is go out to the alley, dig myself a big hole, and copy it there. In German.)

"Well, what's it *about?*"

He looked at Marnie, at her dancer's legs in green

woollen tights stretched straight out in front of her on the floor, and wondered if she really wanted to know.

"I think," he said slowly, reaching over to pour some more wine from the magnum she'd brought over, "it's about learning to keep quiet."

She flashed him an uncertain smile, and he picked up his ragged copy of the *Tractatus* and opened it at random.

"Listen," he said. " 'Propositions can represent the whole of reality, but they cannot represent what they must have in common with reality in order to be able to represent it — logical form. In order to be able to represent logical form, we should have to be able to station ourselves with propositions somewhere outside of logic, that is to say outside the world.' See?"

"I guess not." She detached Hamlin's claws from her mohair sweater.

"Well, I think it's probably like dancing," he said. "No, really. I think you could probably dance it. I think it's a kind of choreography of the mind, of the way the mind works. It's also," he went on, now aware that he was getting quite drunk, "something like a ladder. You're supposed to climb up it, and when you get to the top, you're supposed to step off and kick the ladder over."

She looked at him. "Wittgenstein didn't believe in gravity," he added, by way of explanation.

They were silent for a few minutes. Then: "Hey, your cat's pregnant," Marnie said. "Did you know that your cat was pregnant?"

He was amazed that it hadn't dawned on him earlier. It explained a lot. It explained Ham's (now that he thought about it) utterly uncharacteristic stationing of herself on Marnie's lap, not only this evening but on at least a couple of other occasions he could think of recently. It explained her voracious appetite of late (she had twice raided the garbage bag at night when he'd forgotten to put the lid on the can) and the quirkiness of her jumping up on the counter last week and polishing off the dregs of a can of pineapple tidbits. He'd thought at the time she was getting a bit strange, supposed that it came of living with him. Now he looked at the incipient bulge in her flank as she lay on the floor, and at the prominence of her teats through the soft fur of her underside, and wondered why he hadn't noticed.

"Progeny, eh, Hammer?" he said. "A clutch of little Hamlets. Pied pipers, or maybe I should say poopers. More things to get rid of." But in a way he was pleased. It was a diversion. It was a natural event. It was basic. It provided a focus, in a way, both temporal and practical, a reason for keeping things together and postponing drastic decisions. He was, by now, living like a transient in his own house.

The copying of the *Tractatus* had ceased to be a chore and become more like a form of meditation. It soothed him. The words and logical formulae spilled onto the page, an inexorable stream of strange music. He no longer consciously tried to understand it; he simply copied. At the end, he was confident, enlightenment would come.

The weather grew colder; it snowed, then rained, then snowed again. The apartment, never very bright, took on its winter cast, a cave-like dinginess. By three in the afternoon he had to turn the lights on. At this time last year Janet was sleeping most of the day. He found himself sleeping more; twice he overslept his lecture hour and arrived late to find most of the class had gone. The third time, he called in sick. Bergman, the chairman, summoned him for a consultation with John Bradley, his advisor. Both of them asked him hedgingly personal questions that he answered in monosyllables; he was, he assured them, hard at work on a new approach to his dissertation. No, it was too difficult to explain. Could they see what he had done so far? Michael looked at them doubtfully. It wasn't very readable yet, he said. Maybe in a couple of weeks . . .

You're blowing it. Why don't you just level with them. Ask for a leave-of-absence. Honourable discharge. Or why don't you try to persuade them that simply copying the *Tractatus* is the only legitimate statement one can make on Wittgenstein? That they should accept it as a dissertation? It would save everybody a lot of time and trouble. He felt oddly convinced that Wittgenstein himself, at least, would be open to that, would recognize the validity of what he was doing.

Hamlin recognized it. She had taken, these evenings, to hunching on his desk as he copied, watching his writing-hand intently through half-shut eyes. Sometimes she took a swipe at it, hooking a claw under the skin; he took this to mean he was allowing his attention to wander. As a penance, he would read a page or two aloud to her. At the end of an evening's work, he would stack the latest sheets on top of the mounting pile and Hamlin would get up, stretch, climb onto the stack, and hunker back down, roundly self-possessed, like a bird on its nest. Sometimes she slept there. The bulge in her middle was getting pronounced; it swung from side to side when she walked, and her leaps from floor to desk were slower and less agile.

At the start of December she became restless nights; he'd wake to hear her rummaging in the closet or scrabbling behind the bureau. He foraged a large cardboard carton from the basement and installed it on the closet floor, hoping she'd get the idea. She sniffed at it once or twice, but wouldn't get in. Maybe it wasn't time yet. Or maybe she really did intend to drop her offspring on the linen shelf, nearly six feet off the ground, that she reached by clawing her way up his Army-Navy greatcoat.

What cannot be talked about must be passed over in silence. Faint grey light was just beginning to filter through the dirty window when Michael copied these, the closing words of the *Tractatus Logico-Philosophicus*, onto a clean sheet of yellow newsprint. He blinked; his eyes had the sandy feel that they always got when he stayed up all night. This and the wash of dawn light mixing with the diminished lamp-glow gave him the sense of having come up from under water. Hamlin had disappeared. His knees felt creaky and his back ached.

Air. Give me air. He struggled with the stubborn window-sash till it gave, jerking him back against the corner of the desk. Leaning out on his elbows he took a few gulps of chill morning air. The city smelled of brewery. In the lane below, a grey alley tom with a crooked tail skulked around a corner of the building.

He picked up the overflowing ash-tray on his desk and dumped it out the window, then blew a fine dust of ash off the desk's surface. I should quit smoking, it makes clutter. He switched off the lamp. A sudden gust lifted the top few sheets of the *Tractatus* and scattered them across the floor; drowsily, he crawled about retrieving them. Unnumbered, barely legible, they seemed to have fulfilled their purpose. What cannot be talked about must be passed over in silence. He divided the stack into three equal piles and tore each neatly down the centre. Then he did the same to the half-sheets. He took the bundle of strips into the bedroom, opened the closet, and spread them evenly in the bottom of the cardboard carton. Would that do? After a moment's consideration he took the slip off his pillow — a mono-grammed one Janet had left behind — and smoothed it carefully on top. Then he stretched out on the bed without bothering to undress, kicked his shoes off, and shut his eyes. You forgot to close the window. You'll wake up stiff as a board if you sleep this way. But he didn't move.

Something soft nudged the side of his face; there was a buzzing in his ear. It intensified, subsided, and began again, insinuating, insistent. Now it moved to the other ear. Like a motor; a kind of vibrant hum. He opened one eye and recognized the plume that brushed across his cheek as

Hamlin's tail. She was kneading the pillow with her front paws, purring deafeningly. He opened the other eye. The clock beside the bed said two-thirty; he'd overslept his class again. "Oh, God, Hamlin," he groaned. "I think it's all over for me, this time." He propped himself up on one elbow, slowly becoming conscious that he ached all over. Hamlin continued to knead and purr. Suddenly one of her hind legs shot out stiff behind her and trembled convulsively. The purring redoubled in volume; her eyes looked enormous.

"Hammer?" Realizing with a shock what must be happening, he sat up. What do I do now? I thought they were supposed to quietly disappear and come get you when it's all over. Is she going to have them on the bed?

He got up and opened the closet door. "Kitty," he said softly. "Here, kitty, kitty. Come over here. That's a good girl."

The cat stood in the closet doorway and looked from him to the linen shelf and back again. She crouched as if for a leap up his coat and then seemed to change her mind; to his surprised relief she jumped instead, with a small hoarse meow, into the cardboard box, where she began to knead the pillow-slip. Michael backed out of the closet and went to fill the kettle. There were no cigarettes. He was pulling his boots on when Hamlin reappeared, still purring. She butted her head against his shin, took a few steps toward the bedroom, and stopped to look back at him.

"You *want* me there, Hammer?" He felt an odd mixture of gratification and nervousness as he followed her back to the closet. Hope this isn't going to be too gross. Hamlin jumped into the box, braced herself with her forepaws on the edge, and purred beside his ear as he knelt uncomfortably on the floor. The purring increased in volume; she seemed to rattle with it. Suddenly, without warning, she let out an almost human yell. Michael jumped. The purring resumed as if nothing had happened, but when he leaned to look in the box, there was something dark and wet underneath her. She was nosing it, licking it; then chewing a wet, sticky strand of something — the cord, he guessed. She nudged something else, darkly sticky, like a piece of raw liver, to the edge of the box, touched it with her paw, and began ravenously to eat it. The afterbirth, he realized, aware that he was trembling a little. The cat chewed, purred, chewed, purred. Then she returned to the kitten. Michael could see it moving feebly as she licked it; the blind, almost earless head quivered under the strokes of her tongue. It seemed to be grey all over, though in the murky closet it was hard to tell.

Now he supposed she would settle down to suckle it, but she didn't. She jumped out of the box, cleaned herself briefly, and wandered off in the direction of her food dish, her bulge — only slightly diminished — swaying.

Michael took the opportunity to have a closer look at the kitten. What he saw puzzled him. It was a kitten, all right, it had everything a kitten was supposed to have, but it had something else, too. There was something dark and shiny, a large shapeless bulge, that seemed to be attached to its underside. At first he thought it could be the afterbirth, but he was pretty sure he'd seen Hamlin eat the afterbirth. Was it possible she had accidentally disembowelled the kitten while chewing through the cord? That didn't seem very likely. He was afraid to touch it. By the time Hamlin returned, the kitten was scarcely moving. She nosed it briefly and then jumped out of the box again and meowed at him.

"Hammer." Michael stood up. His foot was asleep. "Hammer, get back in there. I think it needs you. Warm it up, feed it, do something." Then he phoned Marnie. What if she's not in? The extent of his relief when she picked up the phone surprised him. He had never called her before.

He heard her on the stairs moments later, and stepped into the bathroom to splash some water on his face. Marnie came in without knocking, went straight to the closet, and knelt by the box. Hamlin, purring, rubbed against her legs as she crouched there.

"Well, what do you think?"

She turned a puzzled face to him. "I don't know, Michael. It's pretty weird."

"Is it still alive?"

"I can't tell that either. I don't think so."

He said, "I don't know anything about these things, but it occurred to me that it looked like internal organs. As if they were on the outside by mistake."

"Yes, I thought the same thing."

They debated what to do. Hamlin, clearly, wanted nothing to do with the kitten for the moment, but they were afraid if they touched it, she might reject it permanently. On the other hand, without touching it, they couldn't be sure that the thing on its stomach was really attached. Marnie thought maybe they should call a vet; Michael was for waiting a bit. The kitten had not moved for a long time now; they were beginning to be sure it was dead.

Finally he picked it up carefully with the help of a sheet of newspaper, carried it to the light, and confirmed that it was dead. The thing on its underside appeared to be intestines, enclosed in a transparent membranous sac. He wrapped the kitten gently in the newspaper and, not knowing what else to do, left it on the kitchen counter.

After about an hour, Hamlin got back in the box and gave birth to a second kitten with the same improbably deformity. It was smaller, ginger and white, and it moved less than the first. She gave it a perfunctory lick and abandoned it; it lived only a few minutes. Bracing himself, Michael scooped it up and put it with the first.

Marnie followed him into the tiny kitchen and stood beside him as he tucked the newspaper around the two little corpses. Then, timidly, she touched his arm. "It's awful," she said. "It's funny, I don't feel grossed out or anything, just sad. For Hamlin."

He nodded. "I never saw it before — you know? Anything give birth, I mean. I sure wasn't prepared for anything like this."

"I saw a cow once," Marnie said. "On a farm where we stayed one summer when I was twelve. It was weird. It got stuck sideways and the vet had to pull it out with chains."

They went back in the living-room and sat side by side on the floor, not talking much. Hamlin prowled around the apartment, purring loudly, occasionally coming to brush against their legs. She lapped at her water in the kitchen for a long time, but didn't want to eat.

"Do you suppose there'll be any more?" Marnie asked.

"Can't tell." He made some coffee and brought two mugs into the living-room. Then he hesitated. "Would you rather go now? You don't have to hang around if you don't want to."

"No, it's okay," she said. "I feel sort of — " She didn't finish. They looked at each other. The fading light in the apartment brought out odd angles in her face, it was as if he'd never seen it before. She looked drained, remote.

By evening it was apparent that Hamlin wasn't finished and that she was in trouble. She got in her box twice, braced her front paws, purred and strained, but nothing happened. She was trembling and her pupils were dilated. They lifted her into her carrier and called a taxi; Michael carried the dead kittens in a paper bag. In the vet's waiting-room they sat side by side on vinyl chairs under the jumping fluorescent lights and eyed the earlier arrivals: old ladies in slacks with shivering poodles or glowering tabbies in baskets on their laps; a tired-looking man with a scared daughter of about ten hugging a drooling beagle wrapped in a towel; a boy in a frayed college sweatshirt whispering encouragement to the dejected collie under his chair.

Dr. François Pilon unwrapped the newspaper and examined the malformed kittens briefly; then he opened the carrier and lifted a surprisingly docile Hamlin onto the table. He felt her stomach with steady, practiced hands.

"There is at least one more." Michael held Hamlin as the veterinarian plunged a hypodermic into her flank; within minutes her hind leg contracted violently and the third kitten, hairless, half-formed, slid out on the table. The intestinal sac glistened on its underside. It was born dead.

"The condition is called exomphalus," Dr. Pilon explained as he removed his gloves. Hamlin was back in her carrier. "It is a rare one. You see, the intestine are outside the body of the animal. The organs are formed, but the hole is not closed. This happens normally in the last weeks of gestation. With this condition the closure does not occur."

"What causes it?" Michael asked. He cleared his throat; his mouth felt very dry.

The vet smiled gently. "This, we cannot say. Maybe it is genetic. Or it can be sometime the animal ingest something toxic, early in the gestation." He wrote something on a card and handed it to Marnie, who had been standing as if frozen on the other side of the table. "That will be fifteen dollars. If you will kindly pay to the receptionist on the way out? I am sorry."

They flagged a cab on the corner. The hall light in the apartment building was burned out; they groped their way up the stairs in the dark. Marnie came in with him, though he had not asked her to. They let Hamlin out of her carrier and Michael dumped the stale, crusted cat food out of her dish and filled it with fresh. She went straight to it and began to eat, seeming none the worse for the evening's misadventure. Between bites, she purred the same loud, rattling purr.

"Poor cat," Marnie whispered. "I guess up to the last minute I was hoping she'd have one that was — okay. I guess I thought she would."

Michael looked at her. Then, without really knowing why, he walked over and put his arms around her. She seemed to sag against him; turning her face way, she rested her head on his shoulder. He stroked her hair as he would a child's.

"They're not like us," he said softly, wanting to reassure. "They're not people. She doesn't know what's happened to her. It's all hormones, physical changes. She doesn't feel anguish or horror."

"No, I know. It's just — " She shrugged and broke away from him. They stood shoulder to shoulder, arms just touching; a strange awkwardness ensued. Then he said, "Why don't you stay here tonight. If you want to, I mean. Maybe it would be best if you stayed here."

"Yes, I think so," she whispered.

They took off their clothes without speaking, without looking at each other, and got into bed. He reached over to turn off the lamp.

"Michael." It sounded as if she might be crying. He hoped she wasn't crying.

"What's the matter?"

"I just — I want to stay here with you but I don't feel like I could — I mean, after that. It's nothing to do with you, or anything. I mean I like you a lot."

"It's okay, don't sweat it." He felt for her hand under the covers. They lay side by side like statues, hands linked, staring at the ceiling in the dark. In a few moments Hamlin jumped up on the bed, prowled around purring by their heads, and settled herself at last in the hollow between them.

In the morning he scrambled some eggs and made coffee. They ate without saying much, but there was an odd, quiet familiarity between them, a sense almost of resignation. Marnie left immediately for a dance rehearsal, kissing him by the door as an afterthought.

A week went by. He didn't call her, though he thought of it daily. It was as though, having witnessed what they had, he didn't know what he was supposed to feel towards her, what was permitted or required. Hamlin followed him around purring for a few days, unwontedly affectionate, faintly bewildered. By the end of the week her teats had begun to lose their hardness; the incessant purring subsided.

Michael wrote Bergman a letter requesting indefinite leave-of-absence for personal reasons; he also placed an ad in the student paper to sublet his apartment. He was drafting a second ad — "Good home needed for beautiful calico cat, female, part Persian" — the evening Marnie knocked on his door.

"I'm not coming in," she said by way of greeting. "Put your coat on. We're going to a movie."

He obeyed. He was unreasonably glad. "What's playing?"

"*Black Orpheus*. At the Avenue. I've seen it twice, it's wonderful."

He was sure that it was. They clattered down the stairs in their boots and let the double doors clash shut behind them. It was dark out and snowing. "We have to hurry," she said. "It starts in ten minutes."

They strode along arm-in-arm, not quite in step with each other; festoons of Christmas lights swam past him. Snow swirled around the streetlamps; it caught on their hair and in their lashes. Without thinking about it, he began to hum "Kitten on the Keys."

They arrived and found seats just as the lights went down. He eased his arms out of his coatsleeves and shook back his hair; small rivulets of melting snow slid down his face. There was just time to find Marnie's cold fingers in the dark before the movie broke over him like a warm bath.

New Management

SHORTLY AFTER SUNDOWN on the Day of Atonement, that is to say just as the day was formally drawing to its close, Mark Levin clattered down the curved outdoor staircase of his Mile-End flat and headed west towards Benny's Delicatessen to break his fast.

Mark wasn't sure why he'd fasted. He was nearing thirty and had hardly been inside a synagogue since his Bar Mitzvah — and on few enough occasions prior to that, if truth be told. He was a bachelor, for the moment — had lived with a series of women, none of them Jewish, and dated a few that were, but never with matrimony in mind. He had advanced degrees in Russian history, had outgrown the fervour of his Marxist days, made a comfortable living (for a single person) teaching humanities at a private college, and had arranged his life, though not by design, so that he had few occasions to contemplate the fact of his Jewishness. This though in the course of his ins and outs among the neighbourhood shops, he rubbed shoulders daily with bearded and ringleted Hasidim, excused himself squeezing past their wives' double-seater prams in doorways, dodged the street games of their impeccably dressed, Yiddish-speaking children. He looked at them askance from a remove that was not without its proprietary aspect; he was ready to jump to their defence if anybody he knew said anything at all about them, but secretly he thought they were pretty crazy.

He began to pass them now, in little dark clusters, hurrying home from shul to break their own fasts; from their open, lighted doorways he caught an occasional whiff of foods he remembered from when his grandmother was still alive — chicken and beef that fell off the bone at a touch, but had preserved every ounce of their juice and flavour; dense, brown-crusted potato *kugels*, beds of fluffy kasha drenched in rich gravy. In the gathering dark, wafting to him through the cool damp air (it had rained all day, a slow, chill rain — the first rain in a couple of weeks) there was a poignancy to these smells that troubled him. Mark prided himself on his rationality, he mistrusted schmaltz in any disguise, including that most irritating one of no disguise at all; and it was schmaltz that he was smelling now, schmaltz unadulterated and undisguised, the balm of his earliest years. He told himself it was just that he'd been fasting, anything edible would smell poignant when you hadn't eaten for twenty-four hours; and he tried to fix his mind on a Benny's Lean on Rye, with a side order of fries and extra pickle.

Fasting this year had been an odd whim; he wasn't sure what had prompted it. For him even to know it was Yom Kippur was unusual; for close to a decade now, the Jewish holidays had passed him by unnoticed, days like other days. As a child he'd been kept out of school on the High Holidays, "to show respect" was how his mother put it; they'd not gone to synagogue or done anything special to mark the holiday at home, but in their primarily Jewish neighbourhood it "wouldn't have looked right" to send the children to school. In adolescence, for a couple of years, he'd fasted with his friend Davy Cohen, even gone to shul with him; and in college, too, once or twice, in solidarity with other Jewish students in his dorm. But this time — alone — it came out of nowhere. He'd seen a notice regarding the holiday in the newspaper; he'd decided, for once this year, to cancel his classes for the day ("to show respect," he seemed to hear his mother urging) and he'd felt pleasantly absolved of a vague guilt that had nagged him other years, when he'd gone ahead and taught if he had classes scheduled that day. The rest had followed. If he were staying home, it followed that he should fast; his respect shouldn't be a mere formality. He felt good about fasting.

The first yellow leaves were pasted to the wet sidewalk, to the grey wooden stairs of the house-fronts he passed; new ones came down with every gust. A fine mist blurred the streetlamps; the reds and blues of neon along St. Viateur jumped fitfully. Mark lifted his head and breathed deeply the damp air. The day's rain had changed the smell of the city, suddenly brought on a new season; it was strange, it brought the river nearer. It was almost salty, it made him think of coastal cities he'd visited, Vancouver, Boston, cities where you could smell the ocean. But then he was assailed again, those smells, another Hasidic dinner, from an open door of a corner house whose leaning front porch looked as though it was being allowed to rot slowly into the ground.

Mark Levin frowned; he stopped under the corner streetlamp and fished in his pocket for cigarettes and matches. Wind snuffed out his first two attempts to light up; when success came, he inhaled deeply, gratefully, a Craven Blue. It made him dizzy, like a teenager — the fasting, he realized; the first smoke all day, and on an empty stomach. He glanced again at the corner house; a trio of young girls had come out on the ramshackle porch to await relatives. They were dressed alike in those funny, loose, old-fashioned frocks, long white stockings, floppy collars and sleeves; sisters, the oldest maybe seven, the others running close behind. They leaned on the rickety railing and looked back at him with what might have been friendly curiosity; safe behind his cigarette, for no reason that he could have articulated, Mark acknowledged them with a smile and a wave of the hand. They were quaint and pretty and their dinner smelled good and he had fasted this year. But at his gesture of fellowship they froze for a moment; then the youngest whispered to the middle one, he heard them giggle. "Hello," called the middle one in surprisingly bold, ringing tones, not at all shy. "Hello," replied Mark Levin, saluting them again as he walked on. "Hello," they called after him in chorus, and then one of them added, in a voice now suddenly, unmistakeably, derisive, though still coquettish, "Hello, *goy*."

Rapidly Mark strode on, his heart beating a little faster. 'Goy,' they had called him, Gentile; *goy* — for this had he fasted? And was it a matter of ringlets and little hats, then, who could be called a Jew? Was that it? I feel my solidarity with *you*, he thought angrily, I defend *you* when people make fun of you, but you — you don't even acknowledge me as one. And didn't my grandmother light candles, he went on to himself, bemused by his own indignation; and wasn't I Bar Mitzvah, and didn't I go to Israel in '67, even though the war was over by the time I got there and I ended up on a kibbutz picking oranges?

But, of course, they can't tell I'm Jewish by looking, he reflected, so they weren't disincluding me, they simply mistook my identity. And for a moment he felt comforted. But then the thought came, supposing they did know, would it make a difference? Wouldn't they still call him goy? For travelling incognito, for not making sure, as they did, that no one could mistake his identity? And he remembered his friend Elaine, who'd applied for a job teaching math in a yeshiva and lost it to a woman from France. "They'd rather have a non-Jew than a Jew who isn't observant," she'd told Mark. "It's less threatening — it creates less conflict."

Suddenly there came to him very vividly a dream he'd had a long time ago, oh, a decade ago at least, back when he was in college. He was in a small boat with an odd assortment of people, acquaintances and strangers; when he woke, he could not remember who any of them were except for one, a girl he'd dated briefly and had no special feelings for, a slightly stocky Jewish girl with nice but mournful eyes, who'd startled him once by saying, "I like all kinds of people, I like people from all over, but I only feel an *understanding* with other Jews." Cindy, her name was; there were Cindy and him and all these other people, standing in a line along the deck rail; and the captain, there was a captain, was explaining that the boat would soon lose sight of land, and that everyone should be prepared because it would be disorienting — the lake had no horizon, on account of tricks of the light at this latitude.

Then the faint ridge of land disappeared, and the boat seemed as if suspended in a horizonless nothingness of pure, wavering light. Light in perfectly even, mathematical waves. It was beautiful but frightening. There was nothing to distinguish water from sky; all was a continuum of shimmering light, nothing to orient oneself or fix one's sights on. It was beautiful but he felt its potential to become frightening. He felt he had to hang on to the thought that it was beautiful, to keep from being frightened.

And what was that all about, he wondered, and why should I have remembered it just now? Because of Cindy and that thing she said? It must have struck me when she said it, for it to have stayed with me all this time; it's the only thing I can remember her saying . . .

Preoccupied with these thoughts, Mark Levin tossed away his cigarette and pushed through the double doors of Benny's; he slid into a booth, waved away the menu, and ordered a Lean on Rye without looking up.

"*Quoi?*" The waitress seemed new on the job.

"*Un sandwich.* Smoked Meat."

She slapped the menu down in front of him and pointed; he nodded. Then he looked around. The T.V. was going without the sound. Benny wasn't there, but Benny often wasn't there. It was a while, it was well over a year, getting on to two years, since Mark had come in here at all, and Benny hadn't been around much back then. Still, you wondered — could he have retired? Behind the counter were two young men he couldn't remember having seen before, swarthy, with Mediterranean features and slicked-back hair; they looked to be brothers. They were conversing in a language he didn't recognize, not Greek, not Portuguese. A rapid-fire language; he had a fleeting, almost wistful hope that they might be Israeli, but it wasn't Hebrew. Armenian? he wondered.

"What's happened to Benny?" he asked the waitress as she set a glass of water in front of him.

"*Qui?*" She spoke brusquely; she sounded harried.

"Benny. You know, the old man. The owner."

She looked at him sharply and went over to the counter; the men stopped talking and looked at her. She said something he couldn't hear; now they were all looking at him. Then an elderly man in a brown tweed suit, elbows on the counter, half swivelled his stool.

"Benny, the old owner. He means the old owner," he said in a gravelly voice, and swivelled the rest of the way to look at Mark. "New management," he explained, waving at the young men. "Nine, ten months now."

Then Mark noticed — how could he have missed them — the strings of sausage hanging in the window, the lamb and pork halves, reflected in the glass under the fluorescent lights. Below them in the dark pane he saw his own face looking back at him, thin and bearded, brooding, with lines around his mouth he hadn't known were there.

Furniture

WHEN THE TIME CAME for him to leave in the fall, it was
quietly understood that she would take over the house —
furnished as it was, with the things he'd accumulated over
the course of two years, and the lease still in his name till
spring. The house was too good to give up: a corner flat on
a quiet street, with windows facing three ways, large high-
ceilinged rooms, and a ridiculously low rent. She would be
more comfortable there; her own apartment was small and
overpriced, and in any case she had spent most of her time
the past few months at his place.

Besides, it would solve the problem of what to do with
his things. "I'll leave everything here," he told her. "But feel
free to do what you want with it. Things aren't important
— they come to you as you need them. I had nothing when
I came here — don't know where all this came from." And
he told her of how he had left whole houses full of furniture
in other cities, cities all over the continent, places he'd lived
before. "I don't hold with people who say you shouldn't
have things — why shouldn't you have them? Have them
and use them as you need them, but don't let them hang
you up. Pass them to others when it's time to go."

Right up to the last minute she clung to an unvoiced hope that he would change his mind, ask her to go with him, decide to stay himself. It was incredible to her that these months together had changed nothing for him — that he could hold so calmly to what he told her at the outset — told her that first morning, lying at ease in bed beside her, leaning back against the pillows. His eyes, sleepy and warm, were crinkled against the sunlight; his hand rested lightly on her bare arm. "Something you've got to know, Martine — I want to be straight with you. I'm leaving here. In September."

A tiny nerve in her upper lip quivered, but she kept her face composed — looked straight at him, saying nothing. He shifted, reached for the cigarettes on the end-table but thought better of it. After a moment he went on, quietly, "I never came here to stay. I don't stay places. Two years here, it's more than enough. I want to spend some time on the road — alone — find my level again. Things I have to work out for myself. It's just not happening for me here."

He wanted to know, did she understand? Otherwise they should not see each other again, much as he wanted to. She thought and nodded yes — once, then again. Understood. But that quick, grateful pressure of his hand on her arm, she took for a promise of sorts.

After that Dane spoke so seldom of his impending departure that it was easy for her to forget, to shut her eyes against it, hoping it would go away. At first they saw each other once or twice a week, then oftener. They got along well. She saw that he disliked coming to her apartment, so she moved her plants and a few belongings to his place and came there instead. As he had little respect for the social sciences, she shrugged off her work in city planning and kept that part of her life separate from him. He had a simple order of his own, a preferred way of doing things, and this she sought not to disturb, quietly finding her place in it. Though he said nothing, his eyes told her that she had read her cues right, that things were just as he wished between them, and that it meant a lot to him.

Intimacy was in his manner, but not in his words. Once or twice, when her probes were too personal, his face registered a warning; so she pieced his life together from fragments, never by direct questioning. He was thirty-two; his parents were dead. He had a divorced wife and two small sons in Vancouver, an estranged brother in Philadelphia, and an older, married sister in New Zealand. A friend's offer of a job had brought him to Montreal — a replacement contract, teaching drama at a junior college. He needed the money to finish paying for his divorce. All these scraps of information she stored away, completing a picture for herself, as if this would help her to hold him. And every day that went by without mention of his leaving, she counted in her favour.

When his college term ended, she took her vacation and they drove east, camped through the Maritimes, sat in the car with the lights on, late at night, poring over maps. They picked up hitchhikers, met people like themselves who had left the city to buy land, start communes, build houses in the woods. There was talk, intoxicating talk, about survival, eco-systems, synergy, spiritual community; there were gifts of P.E.I. homegrown, parties on the beach. Softened by smoke and wine, Dane spoke of buying land, a farm; he said "we" and she smiled and said nothing, looking into his eyes with new assurance.

So much between them was unspoken, and it seemed to her that she had learned to accept this, to recognize it as a special connection they had formed, a mystical bond, beyond ordinary need for clarification. It was in the way they could laugh together at nothing, a dream he'd had, a fragment of conversation overheard at a truck stop, the swoop of a gull for sandwich leavings. It was how they'd turn to each other at the same moment, sitting by the fire at night, or on a sandstone bluff overlooking the water on a windy day. How his hand would tighten around her shoulder as they strolled along an unpaved road, at the sight of an abandoned farmhouse with a For Sale sign.

Driving back to Montreal, they were silent for long hours. Sometimes as they approached a roadside diner, he'd glance at her inquiringly and she'd nod; without a word they'd get out of the car, stretch their legs, and disappear behind separate doors. She'd emerge to find him seated at a booth, toying with the cigarette papers while he waited for coffee; as she slid in opposite him, they'd look at each other briefly. She waited for his smile: the slow, gentle, faintly tired smile that she took as an affirmation of what had grown quietly between them.

But in August he grew more silent than usual, took to

sitting up late, nights, sorting through bureau drawers, musing over old papers. He filled up plastic garbage bags with things he was discarding, and carried them out to the alley. Often when she came back from work she would find him underneath the car, an array of borrowed tools spread out on the sidewalk beside him; and he would greet her vaguely, without looking up. Sometimes, after supper, he would go out without saying anything and come back at three or four in the morning.

She hid her mounting panic, but he seemed to sense and resent it, avoiding her eyes, snapping at her over trifles. The one time she tried to talk, he cut her short. "I'm not making any statements. It's been so fine with you, Martine . . . don't spoil it now. Let's both of us leave things open. No promises — but trust me a little."

From that point on, they confined themselves to practicalities. She signed "Martine Blondin" beneath "Dane Anderson" on the lease. He rented a U-Haul and helped her move the rest of her belongings out of her apartment, find room for them in the house. Together they painted the kitchen and hall — her choice of colours — and he repaired and fitted the storm windows to be ready for winter. He packed one small trunk of books and papers to be forwarded to him later, in case he decided to stay somewhere awhile.

On their last night they sat for a long time in the living-room in semi-darkness, neither moving nor speaking, their hands linked lightly. The shadows of leaves trembled on the window-screen; lights of passing cars traced the ceiling.

Four candles burned in wine-bottles; now and then a breeze came in and bent the flames.

The candles went out one by one, drowning in their own wax, till only one remained and they watched it together. Wax drops pearled down the sides of the bottle, crackling, clear, stopping halfway down in a milky freeze. The blue flame danced on the lip, ducked down into the mouth and flickered up again. Each time they thought it about to die, it flared orange, fluttered valiantly, stretched upward to a fine still point. Their eyes met over it, startled by the same perception; incredulous, they smiled. They would watch until it went out.

Serious, intent, they leaned together and scarcely breathed. The flame hung on miraculously, now crouched low, now leaping and quivering, as though possessed of a living spirit. Suddenly a paroxysm seized it. The remains of the candle dropped through the neck of the bottle; the flame plummeted like a falling star, glimmering through green glass, and went out. Thick white smoke, like vapour, seeped up and hung ghostly in the mouth of the bottle.

She heard him release his breath and whisper her name. Their hands tightened slowly, held for a long moment, and let go.

He left at six in the morning, in a fine misty rain. The streetlamps glowed palely in the growing daylight; the leaves of the cottonwoods were turning yellow. She stood on the porch, the wind flapping her thin kimono against her legs, and watched the rebuilt Datsun labour around the corner out of sight. Then she turned and went back into the kitchen, shut the door against the draft, flicked off the now superfluous light, and poured herself a second cup of coffee. His empty cup sat opposite hers; his chair was pushed back. She left early for the office, glad that the language she worked in was French — a language he didn't speak, a way of removing herself from him.

On the surface, very little changed in her life. She continued to go to work, she stopped at the usual stores on the way home and bought groceries, fresh rolls, breakfast bacon. Turning the corner she sometimes entertained a thin hope that the Datsun would be parked in front of the house, but as the days went by she refused herself this indulgence.

At the end of two weeks a letter came. The car had made it as far as Sault Ste Marie — better than he'd hoped — and he was thumbing his way on to Vancouver. The weather was bad, the rides few and far between, and he wondered what he was doing there. He missed her a lot. He wanted to see his sons, but after that he didn't know — he might be back in the spring. She folded the letter and carried it in her purse till it was velvety around the edges.

A second letter, a longer one, came at the beginning of October. This one said nothing about coming back. It was full of his experiences, people he'd met along the way, early snow in Alberta and the chance of making some money in Calgary and buying a truck. After that there was a post-card from Mission, B.C. where he was visiting friends; then nothing.

Telephone calls came for him from people she didn't know, mostly women. Some, she guessed by their hesitant, breathless voices, had been his students. It gave her a peculiar satisfaction to tell them that he had left town, that he was not coming back and that he'd left no forwarding address. The silence which usually followed this announcement confirmed suspicions she preferred not to think about. She contemplated changing the phone number, but the thought that he might try to call prevented her.

The gas and hydro bills continued to come in his name and she paid them without changing the account. She found it reassuring, when she picked up mail from the mat, to see his name on an envelope. Other things came for him as well — junk mail, tax forms, bulletins from the college. She put it all in a drawer in the kitchen.

Only one personal letter ever came. This, too, she put in the drawer, but a few nights later she took it out and opened it. She read, "Dear Dane, The Alumni Society forwarded your letter. It sure was a surprise. Hope this reaches you before you leave. I'm in Seattle now as you can see. A lot of water under the bridge. I think of you too — " She crushed the paper in her hand and walked around the house looking for somewhere to stow it. Finally she went outside and poked it down a sewer grate.

Snow fell; the days all ran together. From time to time, separately, friends of Dane's came by to see her. They liked her, and they felt at home in this house where she had changed so little in his absence. She would light candles and bring out the battered enamel coffee-pot, the unmatched cups, the brass dope-pipe; they would sit or sprawl comfortably in low armchairs Dane had removed the legs of, and pass the pipe back and forth, talking dreamily as old albums played over and over on the jerry-rigged turntable. By some tacit agreement they avoided mention of Dane except in passing. One of them she slept with, occasionally, unemotionally.

The telephone call came in mid-winter, waking her rudely in the middle of the night. Heart pounding, she reached over, took the receiver off the hook, and put it down on the pillow. A voice beside her ear whined, "I have a collect call from Dane Anderson in Vancouver. Do you accept charges?"

"Yes," she whispered.

"I have a collet call for anyone there from a Dane Anderson. Do you accept the charges?"

"Yes, I do," she repeated, gripping the receiver. "Dane?"

"Thank you," drawled the operator. There was a click. Then his voice, slow and easy, "Martine?"

"Yes." Her voice was shaking; she laughed at it. "Dane, what's happening? Are you all right?"

"I'm all right — " A short silence. "I'm in Vancouver. Did I wake you or something?"

"It doesn't matter." She reached to turn on the bedside lamp, blinked at the clock. "It's three in the morning." She laughed again.

"I wanted to wait till midnight because it's cheaper then. It's midnight here," he said. "I couldn't remember whether

Montreal was ahead or behind."

"Ahead. I can never remember things like that either." Why are we wasting words, she thought, and said impulsively, "Dane, it's awfully good to hear your voice."

He gave a short, embarrassed laugh. "It's good to hear yours. I guess that's why I called. Sure wish I had something good to say."

"Aren't things working out?"

"No." Another short silence. "Are you sure you want to hear all this?"

His story came out in bits and pieces. He'd been in Vancouver a month, living in a used truck he'd bought in Calgary. The truck was a write-off; he'd lost a lot of money on it. He'd seen his kids a few times, but his ex didn't want him around, wouldn't let him see them outside the house. It was a bind; she didn't trust him, the boys sensed it, and she refused to reason or compromise. She just wanted him out of the picture, and he didn't have the energy to fight her. There seemed no point in sticking around — only, on top of everything else, he'd run out of money.

She thought quickly and said, "I can send some."

A pause. "Only if you think you can afford it." But he gave her a bank account number.

They spoke of possibilities. He could go across to Vancouver Island and live on the beach for a while; it would clear his head. He'd heard there were places to squat — empty fishermen's shacks, driftwood houses hippies had built and abandoned. And work: he might be able to get on at a sawmill. Maybe she could take her vacation in the spring and join him there, and they'd take a train back to Montreal together. It sounded good to him. But he didn't know; he'd thought of trying to get on a boat for New Zealand — he'd worked on boats before. He felt so down, seemed like the thing might be to go somewhere else and start all over again. His sister was in New Zealand.

She said, "Shouldn't you build on what you're sure of, instead of just running? You know you had something good here." And he was silent, thinking. "You may be right." Finally they settled it that he would mull things over and call her back in a few days.

The receiver was warm when she put it down. She lay still for a few minutes, listening to the tap of ice-laden branches against the window, and then switched off the lamp, turned over on her stomach, and slept like a baby.

In the morning she wired him two hundred dollars. The second phone call never came.

Winter hung on. Martine could not have said, would not have said, that at any point she stopped waiting. For a time it was at the back of her mind to try to contact him, through the bank, but a kind of lassitude overtook her whenever she sat down to write the letter, and always she shoved it to the back of the desk after a sentence or two, telling herself she'd finish tomorrow. The flat was gloomy and peaceful; when she wasn't at work, she slept a lot, and otherwise occupied herself with things that didn't demand much — re-potting the house plants, sewing new buttons on a sweater. It occurred to her that she might rearrange the furniture, but always this took the form of standing in the middle of a room, considering the possibilities until her head felt tired, and finally deciding to leave it for another time.

At last came those days Montrealers wait for, days of falling water and soft air, people at windows, on balconies, doors flung open to air the closed flats. All afternoon the alley rang with the sound of shovels, chopping and scraping. There were new leaves on the philodendron, faint squares of evening sun on the kitchen wall. Energy stirred in Martine; she took the rugs out and beat them over the balcony rail, washed all the windows, took the curtains down and laundered them.

In May an architect named Lewis Brandon rented the flat above hers. She knew him slightly; she had done consulting for a partner of his in the past. He took the outside stairs two at a time, was given to wearing outlandish ties, and had a booming laugh that she found infectious. If his "Say, haven't we met somewhere?" was self-mocking, his eyes were friendly.

From conversations on the stoop, in the lengthening twilights, they progressed to occasional dinners together; then to an easy, neighbourly back-and-forth between houses. Lewis was intrigued by the potential of their building; he wondered if he could interest her in a co-proprietorship. The neighbourhood was going to become fashionable, he said; it was happening in cities all over the States. The building was of sound construction; if they bought now, they couldn't lose. He had novel, wacky ideas for renovations.

By summer he was spending his nights downstairs and they were drafting floor-plans together, debating the virtues of an open staircase between the two levels. In the meantime they bought antique furniture, a brass bedstead, a roll-top desk, to complement the pieces he'd already brought down from upstairs, relics of a marriage his wife had walked away from "lock, stock, and barrel," he told her, to go live in a shack in the woods with a rock musician and his entourage.

She helped him carry the old furniture out to the alley: the legless stuffed chairs, the Salvation Army bureaus, the mattress and box-spring set on cinderblocks. "Hippie gypsy stuff gets me down," Lewis said. "Why are you living like this, Martine — you're a professional woman, it's not your style."

She talked more, and bought herself a new wardrobe. She quit smoking and enrolled in a furniture restoring course. They took their vacations together in August and flew to England, where they met up with his brother and sister-in-law and cycled through the Lake District. Pedalling like a maniac, Lewis sang love-songs in a theatrical baritone and rolled his eyes at her; she laughed and blushed and told him he was crazy.

The deal on the house was closed before winter. At a party to celebrate, a woman who had gone to school with Lewis and who now taught graphics at a junior college mentioned that a former colleague of hers, Dane Anderson, had once lived on this street. She thought it might even have been this building. Had they ever met him?

Perched on an arm of Lewis's chair, leaning one elbow lightly against his shoulder, Martine laughed. "That con man. He owes me two hundred dollars," she said.

A Minor Incident

FOR A FEW YEARS beginning around when I was twelve, my father worked for a Jewish organization, a branch of it devoted to fighting anti-Semitism. To his desk came samples of printed materials against which complaints had been lodged; he had to read these and decide what action, if any, need be taken — he was a sort of filter for hate literature. Sometimes he brought it home with him in the evenings. I remember a kind of pained face he'd have, like the face of someone who has been walking all day in shoes that are too tight, and whose feet have blistered; and he might call to me from his desk in the alcove, when I was doing my homework at the dining-room table: "Esther. Come here, I want you to see something. I want you to read this. Look, look what they say about us, terrible things . . . look . . ."

But I would not; instead I'd gather up my books without a word, and go to my room and shut the door, clenching and unclenching my hands; would he call me again? would he insist? If he did, my mother might protest to him, in a low voice, in Yiddish which I did not understand; and he would reply audibly, in English, "She's old enough. She should see it. She should know."

I do not remember being told about the Holocaust, not

when, nor by whom, though it must have been one of them, my father or my mother, who told me, before it was called the Holocaust, before it had a name attached to it whereby it could be handled, contained, dismissed. I do know that only a few years elapsed between the time when, waking from nightmares, I was reassured that there were no wicked witches, that there weren't any monsters, that I didn't need to be afraid because there were no such things, they were just "made up" — and the time when I knew that men in uniforms, ordinary human beings, had dashed out the brains of babies against concrete walls before their mothers' eyes, and then shot the mothers dead; and that this was not a bad dream, not a made-up story, but was the truth and had really happened. Who could accept that and need to hear more? The one image contained the Holocaust for me; in it I felt my knowledge to be complete. The rest was numbers. Say it isn't true? Say it didn't happen *really*? No, it really happened. It happened over and over.

I know now, too, that the years when I lay awake in the dark, fearful of witches, were years when the full extent of the horror was still being uncovered; in our house, years of hushed conversations in Yiddish and rustling newspapers, radio babble, grownup talk behind closed doors. My grandmother was alive, then, and lived with us; I remember her room at the end of the hall, with a smell all of its own that permeated everything in it, the maroon plush chair, the chenille bedspread, the patterned Indian rug. She had her own radio, an enormous one with a wicker front, on a shelf above the bed; she had hatboxes in the closet in which were

hats of crumpled felt garnished with glazed wooden cher-
ries, curled black plumes, pearl-tipped hat pins; in her
closet, too, there hung old nylons stuffed at the bottom with
clove and dried orange peel; on her bureau was a glass bowl
filled with rose petals. I remember that every once in a
while, my mother would call her to the telephone in a tense,
urgent tone, and with one hand to her heart she would go;
the conversation that followed would be a trading of names,
of people I did not know and of what I later realized were
towns in Galicia; yes, she would say then, yes? No. No. No.
And she would shake her head at my mother, who hovered
listening. No. No. Her face would slacken, she would wish
the caller good health in Yiddish, and good luck. "A different
Charney," she would say, putting the phone down. "Not
related." It was her brother she was hoping to hear from,
or have news of. People with the same name, arriving in
new cities, would do that then — look up the name in the
telephone book, call each listing, seeking family connec-
tion, word of relatives. They would look up every spelling.
Calls came to us from Charneys, Cherneys, Chierneys. To
no avail.

Years passed before I understood the significance of those
phone calls. That Gran hoped to hear from her brother, yes;
but not why; not what might have become of him, what was
more likely with each passing day to have become of him.
Years, before I realized what had happened to Gran's sister,
the one I knew I was named for. The sister Gran only ever
described to me as the small girl whose hair she, Gran, had
braided each day, as she now braided mine: Esthie, Gran's

littlest sister, still a young girl when Gran came to Canada. Years, before I connected the Holocaust with my family, in a moment of shocked comprehension. That was a connection they never made for me, and why was that? A question I've never answered. There are many such questions from my childhood. The question about Mrs. Howick is one.

When I was twelve my best friend was Rhoda Kendal, quiet like me, studious and shy. We were friends more by circumstance than by our choosing, both of us having transferred from other schools (I in fourth grade, she in fifth) at the age by which girls have formed tight bonds and cliques and are not easily receptive to newcomers. I made no friends in my first year at Wilchester School, and I knew what that felt like, so when Rhoda showed up in my class the next year and I saw her standing alone and diffident in the schoolyard, I took her under my wing. She was a sweet-natured girl with a round smooth face, placid features, and dove-soft black hair that waved. She had an air about her, among the harder-edged, more socially conscious girls, of still being a child, somehow untouched by sophistication; she seemed defenceless to me in her pleated, regulation tunic — a style the other girls, myself included, had discarded in favour of the 'A-line' pleatless tunic older girls at our school were permitted to wear.

My own defences were already in place. Close on the realization that I would not be invited into the circle, at Wilchester, came the realization that I did not want to be. I signified this by fastening my pleatless tunic with the old regulation two-button belt, declining to purchase from the office the long, shiny-threaded sash the other girls rushed, thrilled, to trade theirs for. I continued to clump around in navy-blue Oxfords even after the principal, badgered by mothers of unhappy girls, conceded to allow an alternative, more stylish shoe. In this I differed from the two or three other loners in my class: Donna, the only Gentile girl; Brina who had a mysterious illness that absented her for weeks at a time; Jana who was cross-eyed and came to school with egg on her blouse. They, like the rest, opted for sashes and loafers, hoping thus to avoid becoming targets for whispering.

I for my part might be ignored, but I was not whispered about because my marks were too good. I did not strain for this. It was my luck, I was so constituted, that term after term, effortlessly, I led the class; and it was also my luck that Wilchester was a place where that counted.

Rhoda studied much harder than I did and got "Very Goods" and "Goods" where I got "Excellents." It was indicative of her nature that she did not in the least resent me for this, but wholeheartedly admired me and exulted in my successes as if they were her own. "Gee, you make me sick!" she might say, looking at my report card, but she couldn't stop smiling. The other girls who rushed over to compare their marks with mine, subject by subject, said flattering things to me, but their voices betrayed them, barely masking bitter envy.

As my marks protected me from being targeted, so being my friend protected Rhoda. By seventh grade we were inseparable. We spent recesses together, griping about Home Economics, discussing which girls were "boy crazy." On Saturdays we exchanged our books at the library and rode the bus home to her house or mine, giggling too loudly, dropping potato chips in the aisle. At the end of the day, we would walk each other "half-way home," and the half-way might stretch to all the way, then, "I'll walk you half-way home," till it was dark out and we were giddy with the silliness of it. Looking back on it, I think that if Rhoda had not come late to Wilchester and had not met me first of all, she might have become one of the crowd — she had it in her to fit in — whereas I, even had I not come late, would have remained singular and apart. But Rhoda had a loyal heart, and though she ditched her pleated tunic and succumbed soon enough to the sash and loafers, she was staunchly my friend and stuck by me.

Rhoda's parents had been in the camps. I didn't know this at the time; I'm not sure how I know it now. Somebody must have told me, long afterwards — perhaps my mother, perhaps Rhoda herself when we ran across each other again, years later, in graduate school. There was little to show it. They had a home like other homes in that neighbourhood, a brand-new, fashionable split-level, white rugs, sunken living-room, sofas in plastic slipcovers. It was much fancier than my parents' house; the hall floor was parquet instead of vinyl tile; the bedrooms had wall-to-wall carpeting. In the bathroom a basket by the sink contained coloured, scented soap puffs for visitors; I had to ask what they were. Everything was always immaculately clean and tidy; Rhoda and her younger brother and sister, who were twins, were generally not allowed in the living-room. It was a sharp contrast to my house, where a comfortable level of clutter prevailed and everything — furniture, flooring, fixtures — had a well-used, time-worn look.

I preferred for Rhoda to come to my house because I never felt entirely comfortable in hers. Her parents (when they were around, for both worked) spoke Yiddish most of the time; their English was poor, formal, and thickly accented. About them I felt a foreignness, an apart-ness, that I could not read or gauge. Rhoda's mother was not friendly like mine. She would smile at me and say hello when she came in, but she never conversed with me or drew me out, as my mother did with the friends I brought home, and she never sat down to chat with us when we fixed ourselves snacks in the gleaming kitchen; instead she would retire to another room. Once, I confessed to Rhoda that I did not feel welcome in her house, that I thought her mother disliked me; but Rhoda, stunned, told me her mother liked me very much and was happy she, Rhoda, had me for a friend. "She's shy, Esther," she told me, "and she thinks her English is bad. Maybe she's afraid you'll laugh at her. I tell her all the time how brilliant you are — "

Of Rhoda's father I have only one clear memory, and it strikes me now as being an odd one. It is of a hot spring afternoon when I arrived at the house to call for Rhoda; we were going somewhere together, I don't remember where, and as I turned up the walk, Rhoda called to me from her bedroom window, "I'll be down in a sec, I'm just changing."

To pass the time, I strolled around the side of the house to look at the lilacs, and came suddenly upon her father on a ladder in the driveway, shirtless, painting the garage door. He had a cap on, and for a moment I thought he was a hired worker; then he looked up from beneath the visor and smiled at me, an oddly warm, sad smile that crinkled the corners of his eyes. He was amused to see that I had not recognized him, and motioned me nearer. "Esther. So, Esther. You like my hat?"

I felt awkward and shy. It was the first time I had seen him alone, or exchanged more than a word or two with him. I can't remember the conversation we had there, in the sunny driveway, with faint breezes wafting the smells of lilac and wet paint; but I remember that the tone was kindly, gentle, sad, and oddly intimate. "It's hard, to be a Jew," I remember him saying to me in his European accent, slowly shaking his head (and my sudden, forlorn sense of discomfiture) — "You know what they say, Esther? It's hard to be a Jew."

What was the context? I cannot at all remember. And did this scene take place before, or after, the incident with Mrs. Howick? That, too, evades me.

Seventh Grade was at that time the final year of elementary school, a year in which teachers strove to prepare students for the comparative rigours to come. Our teacher, Mrs. Howick, was strict and uncompromising, but scrupulously fair. She was a short woman in her mid-forties — the bigger girls already had the edge on her — but she commanded respect in every fibre by the way in which she planted herself at the front of a classroom: square posture, legs placed slightly apart, chin erect, hands on hips. She wore pleated skirts, high-necked blouses, dark support hose, "sensible" shoes. No jewellery, no perfume — indulgences of the younger teachers on staff. Her hair, a nondescript light brown as yet unmixed with grey, was centre-parted and cut short, it stood out a little from her face, giving her a severe yet slightly dowdy appearance.

I liked her well enough. She had a brisk, animated classroom style, could be salty, was not boring, gave a reasonable amount of homework, and expected us to deliver, without coddling. Her digressions, when she digressed, were interesting. She quickly recognized my abilities and acknowledged me matter-of-factly, without effusions; she also gave me to understand that it was the thoughtfulness of my answers, rather than the correctness, that she valued. "Think, think, think," she used to exhort us, "don't let anybody else do your thinking for you." Or sometimes, if she asked for a show of hands on who agreed with a particular answer: "What are you looking around at your neighbour for? I'm asking what *you* think! *You*! Never mind the others! Else you're nothing but sheep." Her words were often accompanied by so vigorous a tapping of her pointer against the blackboard or floor that the wooden stick would snap in two, the broken end bouncing off somebody's desk to the accompaniment of stifled giggles.

The comparing of marks, whenever a test was given back, was something that evoked equal vehemence from her. "Keep your paper to yourself. What do you care what *she* got? 'What did you get, what did you get?' " (she mimicked, in mincing tones). "Is that all that matters to you? Look at your *own* paper! *Read* the comments on it — do you think I write them to amuse myself? Look at your mistakes, *learn* something!" And shaking her head in exasperation: "It's marks, marks, marks, with you people — that's all you're interested in. Just like with your parents it's money, money, money. Who's got the most — isn't that true? Today it's marks, marks, marks, and when you grow up, it'll be money, money, money."

One afternoon in midwinter, as I was getting my books together to leave, she spoke to me from her desk in an uncharacteristically personal tone. "Esther, do you have a few minutes to spare? Please stay behind. I want to talk to you about something."

My heart lurched for a second, but my conscience was clear. Maybe she had plans for me for the school concert. Maybe she wanted me to help her with something. Wondering, I followed her out of the classroom — away from a group of girls who were staying for detention — and down the hall a distance. "Esther," she said then, in a confidential voice, putting a hand on my shoulder, "I don't know if you've heard that I've been accused of saying things against Jews." Her eyes looked straight into mine, transfixing me. I shook my head; I was tongue-tied.

"Esther," she repeated. "You're Jewish. You're my brightest student. Please tell me. Have you ever heard me say anything against Jews?"

Again I shook my head. My heart was pounding; I didn't know why. It flashed through my mind that I had never thought of Mrs. Howick as being non-Jewish, or as not being Jewish. I had never thought of the student body at Wilchester, a Protestant school, as being almost all Jewish, even though I knew that in our class, only Donna wasn't, and that on Jewish holidays the handful of students from all grades who showed up were pooled in one classroom and had Art all day; Donna had told us.

"Esther, you know what I say when people in the class start comparing their marks — that they want more marks just like their parents want more money? Tell me the truth. When I said that, did you ever think that I was speaking against Jews?"

No, I had not thought so, I said, completely taken aback.

"Good. I'm glad. Well, dear, some people have thought so. Your friend Rhoda mentioned it to her parents, and her parents complained. They brought it up at the P.T.A. meeting last week, and some parents were upset and called the principal." She tapped the squat heel of her shoe against the shining floor; I saw that the edges of her hair were quivering. "Esther, you know that it was *people* I was talking about, not just Jews, but the kind of person who is always wanting more than the next one; you know some people are like that, don't you?"

"Yes," I said. The tone of entreaty in her voice dismayed me.

"I wanted to ask *you*, because you're a very intelligent girl, and very mature, and because I know you and Rhoda are friends. Maybe you'll talk to her about it. Explain to her that I didn't mean it that way. Will you do that for me?"

I said, "I'll try," and she patted my shoulder, gratefully, and said, "Good girl," and then I left.

That was the end of it; there was no sequel. The episode blew over without further ado; presumably, apologies were made, and the matter was allowed to drop. I did talk to Rhoda, but I don't remember what we said — only that it was a little uncomfortable, a little strained. I think she felt pulled between respect for her parents and loyalty to me; that she neither challenged my opinion nor concurred; but I don't remember. I never mentioned the affair to my own parents, who had little use for the P.T.A. and doubtless had not attended the meeting in question. At the end of the year, Rhoda and I went off to separate high schools and gradually, as our lives diverged, lost touch with each other.

But I still sometimes think about Mrs. Howick. Though I shovelled it under at the time, I know that something opened up beneath me, that afternoon in the dim-lit school corridor, like a section of floor caving in. I see her plain, earnest, sometimes sardonic face; I remember that I liked her, and that she liked me. I hear her voice reiterating the offensive phrases and I wonder: Was it a slur, or wasn't it? And was it fair of her to ask me to decide? I could not argue with her observation as it applied to my school and neighbourhood: the kids were as a rule competitive and pushy for marks; the parents were typically brash, upwardly mobile suburbanites of the fifties. But what gave her the right to say it, and *for whom* was she saying it? "You people," she called us. And what was she asking me to uphold — the thoughtfulness of her statement, or the correctness of it? What unexamined premises of hers did my answer endorse? In retrospect I know that even as I gave her what she wanted, even as I said I had not taken her remark to be a slur, I began to wonder whether it had been; and over the years, off and on, I have gone on wondering.

At first what I wondered about was simple: if I liked her, how could she be an anti-Semite? But if she was an anti-Semite, how could I like her? Later, painfully, having allowed that both could be the case, I wondered which of us I had let down the most.

I remember coming late out of school, that winter dusk, and trudging across the empty schoolyard alone, over the bumpy, frozen crust of old footprints. Rhoda had not waited for me; there was no point, as we walked home in opposite directions. I remember how it began to snow lightly as I reached the gate, and how the snow fell thicker and thicker, in swift dizzying flakes, across my path home.

Première Arabesque

WHEN SHE HEARD THE CAR pull into the driveway, Norma Greenberg jumped up from the Steinway baby grand and made a show of tidying some magazines on the sofa end-table. But her father wasn't taken in; he was at her even before he had his coat off.

"You've been at that piano all morning, haven't you, Norma. I thought you had exams to study for this week."

The Bach prelude which had continued to play in her head faltered and lost its direction. It didn't belong here, in the huge living-room with the beige shag carpet, the upholstery in see-through slipcovers, the fringed lampshades and planters spilling over with plastic ivy. She shut her eyes for a moment, but when she opened them the room swam horribly back into focus. Beyond the draperies, rain dashed the glass of the patio doors.

"And what are all those records still doing out of their jackets? I told you to put them away yesterday."

Steadying her voice, she said, "I had to practice, Daddy. I have a lesson today. Mr. Schwartz says before my lesson I should always — "

"Oh, Mister Schwartz, Mister Schwartz. What is he, a god or something. Mister Schwartz says, so she does. Her mother says, her father says, that's a different story . . . this is what my money is paying for . . ." and the voice went on, climbing in pitch in a way that made her numb with hatred, as he slammed about the house. Norma had ceased to listen; she moved silently down the hall to her bedroom, clicked the door shut behind her, and sat down on the corner of her bed — sat there quite still, with one hand pulling idly at a loose thread in her bedspread — while she stared out at the wet patio stones, the painted deck chairs, the lone half-bare sapling at the back of the garden. In the next room her brother's transistor radio bleated, "We-Like-To-Look-After-You, At The Roy-oy-oyal Ba-ank!"

"Norma!" Her mother, this time. "Lunch is on the table. Come eat something before you go. And call Steven, okay?"

. . . *Norma doesn't go out. No, if she had it her way, she'd sit at that piano all day . . . I don't know what to do with the girl . . .*

What do you mean, you're not going? Of course you're going. It's Judy's Sweet Sixteen, *honey! She's your best friend! . . .*

Norma, look what you're doing to your bedspread!

"Norma?"

"I heard you, Mummy. I'm coming."

She banged much louder than necessary on her brother's door, and then ducked into the bathroom, stuck her hands under the cold tap for a second or two, and dried them on her skirt on her way to the kitchen. There were party sandwiches on the lunch counter — little triangles of soft white bread, stale at the edges and soggy with mayonnaise. Salmon, egg, and cheese.

"Left over from the Sweet Sixteen," said Mrs. Greenberg, with a brief significant look at Norma. "Judy's mother brought them over." She poured ginger ale into four tall glasses and pushed them across the counter.

"Did you wash your hands?" asked Mr. Greenberg. Norma said "Yes" with such vehemence that he was nonplussed, and turned instead to her brother. "What about you, Steven, did you wash your hands?"

Steven said "Um." This by way of assent; he was ten and had learned to affect for such purposes a totally expressionless face.

"You did not," said Mr. Greenberg. "Let me see them."

"Oh, jesus, Harold, they're not babies. Leave them alone."

They ate and drank in silence. Norma felt that Steven was looking at her, and when she looked up, he was — blankly, with his mouth slightly open. She looked away irritably and then back again. His position and expression had not changed. She glared. Finally she burst out, "What are you staring at me for, Steven!" and his eyes registered a quick change — startlement, followed immediately by stubborn indifference, and he looked at the wall instead, whistling quietly to himself through his teeth.

The doorbell chimed. "It's the paper-boy," said her mother. "Get it, will you, Norma? The money's on the hall table."

Lately she had hated to answer the doorbell. It wasn't something she could explain, but it was awful to see someone standing there, waiting. Watching, smug and superior, from the doorway, while she fumbled around looking for the money — a pencil — a parcel her mother was return-ing. *Norma, didn't you hear the doorbell? Well, get it, will you? Why must your mother always get up?*

The paper-boy was a skinny redhead in a raincoat much too big for him. He had that watery, myopic look about the eyes some red-haired people have — it made her want to put her hands up to her own eyes. A gust of wind came into the hall, and a smell of wet newsprint. She thrust the crumpled bill into his hand, took the damp paper, and began to close the door — caught a look at his astonished face — "Hey, wait," he said, banging on it with his fist, "Wait!" She opened the door with her heart pounding strangely — "You forgot your change," he said.

Her mouth formed the word "Oh" and she took it from him — shut the door again — squeezing the handful of quarters and nickels tight in her fist. A familiar confusion held her to the spot; she stood uncertainly in the hall, thinking, trying to remember. Wasn't there something spe-cial today, that she had been feeling good about? Yes, there was. It was Saturday. Her piano lesson. Not Sunday, when she cleaned her room and washed her hair and did home-work. Relieved, she spilled the fistful of coins onto the glass tabletop and went to gather her piano books together.

She stood at the piano a few moments, silently fingering the opening of the Debussy Arabesque. She would not play aloud now because of *him*. But the keys were cool and smooth under her fingers, and she knew, by a certain weighted calmness in her hands and arms, that it would be a good lesson.

"If you want a lift, get ready, Norma," called her father. "I've got to be back at work at one." He came into the hall and stood watching her put her coat on. She didn't look at him.

Outside, the rain was like a fine spray, cold and gusting. The blue station wagon sat waiting in the driveway. The cold seat; doors slammed; the engine starting up — then the meaningless, erratic tic, tic of the windshield wipers.

As the car zipped through puddles, along wet pavement that gleamed the grey-white sky back at itself, Norma felt the double edge of her father's silence. Without looking at him she knew that his eyes were narrowed in concentration at the road, but that his thoughts were elsewhere, speeding. And she wondered, as she sometimes had before, what it was about a person — a simple, breathing lump of human matter, occupying just so much physical space in the universe — what it was that made the difference. Why this man at the wheel, for example, this stoutish man now scarcely taller than she was, with hairless scrubbed hands and short thick fingers — her father — should have an effect on her of constraining her breathing, slowing her brain, numbing the surface of her skin. And why, because it was the two of them here in the car, the air should be thick and charged, like the air between the same poles of two magnets you try to force together. An invisible field of resistance, pushing apart in dark, velvety waves.

Easy and silent, the car rode through empty streets — past square white houses with gleaming picture windows and half-drawn curtains, past broad paved driveways and closed garage doors, treeless lawns, ranks of low, pruned shrubbery. And somewhere there is a huge tangled garden, a fountain cluttered with leaves; somewhere an upstairs room lined with books (soft colours of old bindings under lamplight) and a window looking out into a tree. Someone leans out there, breathing the smell of wet bark, hearing the creak of branches . . . someone shuts his eyes and imagines a girl he could really talk to, a girl who would sit beside him on the edge of the fountain, trailing her fingers in the water . . . (But how do I know that? How can I know?)

Her father cleared his throat. "So how are the lessons progressing, daughter?" he asked.

She kept her face averted, looking out the window. The car took a turn into another section of town: stores, striped awnings, bright-lit windows. People walked here, under gaily coloured umbrellas.

She said, "Fine, I guess."

One block. Two. Then a red light. He was waiting. It was his way of saying he was sorry, she knew. He wanted it to be all right between them now, he wanted to show her he was interested. No, he wanted her to go along with the *pretense* that he was. He wanted her to talk to him, but she couldn't.

The light changed. "Costing me enough," he muttered.

A slow smoulder, it was almost a relief, began inside her. "Don't pay for them, then. I'll go to work."

"Go on," said her father almost mildly. "I'd like to see you go to work. Might do you some good. Never have a civil word to say to anybody in the house — sit on your fanny daydreaming about your Mr. Schwartz . . ."

Tears stung her eyes. (*Don't.*) But her voice shook all the same. "*Keep* your money, Daddy, if all you're using it for is something to hold over me."

"Now don't give me any lip, because I'll do that, Norma. I'll do that and you can say goodbye to your piano."

Tell him. Go ahead, tell him.

She told him. "Mr. Schwartz said he would go on teaching me for free, if you ever cut off the lessons."

The car lurched forward, throwing her against the seat.

"Oh, he did, did he?" said her father. And his voice was like elastic stretched to breaking. "For free? Is that what he said? Or did he have some other kind of payment in mind, maybe?"

It took her an instant to believe what she heard. Then she screamed, "Daddy, *shut up*, why can't you just *shut up*!" And she saw his face go suddenly slack, saw the twitch in his cheek, and knew they had taken it too far this time, both of them, beyond recrimination or retreat, beyond hope of anything but silence to repair. He doesn't mean it, she thought, he hates himself for saying it, he hates himself anyway. He hates his life, he has nothing. And I have this, that's what he can't stand. But knowing it was no help. It was easier not to know it.

Tic, tic went the windshield wipers. Her shoulders shook, the tears streamed down her face, but without a sound. He let her out on the corner of Mr. Schwartz's block, and she ran up the street, crying silently, hugging the pile of frayed piano books.

Mr. Schwartz lived in the middle building of the shabby brick apartment block, on the third floor. In the lobby she stopped to pull herself together; she could hear the piano even from downstairs — a phrase of Chopin, tossed back and forth between pupil and teacher. First slow and faltering, in the middle register; then light, effortless — like a child's laugh — in the treble. Again. And again. It stopped as she reached the landing, and she heard the familiar murmuring voice behind the loosely latched door of Apartment 32. Sounds that absolved and restored her, that gave her back to herself. She paused there, listening, pushing the wet hair back from her face, adjusting her skirt.

One of the children answered to her knock, admitting her into the dingy hall and the close, turgid atmosphere of the house. In the dimness she could not be sure which of the three, or was it four, Schwartz children it was. They were all small for their age, with dark hair falling in their eyes, and they seemed always to be in pyjamas. They would greet her with an impersonal "Hi" if they said anything at all, and then, skidding on the bare floor in socks, they would melt back into the shadows, disappearing down the narrow hall intent on their own business.

"Norma?" he called. "Take a seat, okay? I'll be with you in a moment." And the voice resumed its patient murmuring, punctuated by brief, bright outbursts from the piano.

She sat at the telephone stand, opening and closing her hands in her lap, and her eyes grew accustomed to the murk. Took in, again, the grubby finger-marks on the walls and door frame, the warped greyish floorboards, the pile of mismatched rubber boots in the corner. A doll without arms, fringed with dust, stuck out from under the radiator — it had been there for weeks. There was a magazine fallen down behind her chair, a picture book with its cover torn off; and on the table beside her an accumulation of mail, unopened for days.

In the front room the lesson continued. Now and then she could make out a word, a phrase — ". . . from the shoulder . . . whole arm . . . now *release* . . . that's it. You've got it." But the words didn't matter. It was the voice that mattered, the rise and fall of that quiet voice, soberly explaining, revealing . . . By the voice alone she could understand all that was happening in that room. What was happening was important — was good. Time stopped for it; worlds hung on it. The weight of an arm, the feel of a key beneath a finger — even one clear tone, struck in its fullness, contained the whole pattern. And this knowledge was a secret, passed down in hushed tones on Saturday afternoons, in rooms that smelled of rain on dusty window-sills.

— now lanky Harvey hovered in the doorway, Harvey with tooth braces and kind troubled eyes. "Do you want me to start on the Franck this week? . . . yeah, okay . . . no, I got a dentist appointment Wednesday. Thursday? Yeah, all right. Four o'clock."

Mr. Schwartz, in baggy trousers and a torn shirt open at the neck, waved her into the front room. The door banged shut behind Harvey and immediately opened again of its own accord. "Damn door," said Mr. Schwartz. "Play some exercises or something, okay Norma? I've got to grab something to eat . . . how are you today anyway?" He was out of the room without waiting for an answer, only to poke his head back in momentarily. "*Who* are you today?" he added, slyly, and disappeared down the dark hall.

This room — this room in which it seemed perpetually autumn — answered the question for her. Today, now, I am this room. I am the rug on the floor, its pattern rubbed out, pile worn to the bare threads in places. I am the small window, looking out onto an inner court, admitting little light. . . I am the wet dust on the sill. I am the brass floorlamp spilling its light on the piano keys, I am the piano keys — still, waiting keys — the solemn alternation of black and white. I am each bubble in that glass of stale water on the piano, that shimmers a little in the lamplight; I am every raised ring on the wood where glasses have stood before. The bare walls, the shadows of dried leaves overflowing a huge vase in the corner, the piles of books on the floor . . . I am this room in which what was supposed to be temporary, somehow stayed that way — a room moved into in haste, years ago, where life resumed so quickly, so fully, that there was no time for things, mere things, to intrude. The curtains, the bookshelves, are plans become sufficient in themselves. The window remains bare. The books are on the floor.

Norma raised her arms and let them drop into a deep, ringing chord. She felt the resonance in every finger. Rest; prepare; fall-to-the-bottom-of-the-key. The room receded.

When Mr. Schwartz came back, moving hastily, balancing plates, his cup trilling in its saucer, she had taken the progression through six keys. He set his toast and coffee down on top of the piano and stood back, watching her. "Good. You've got it, you don't need me for that. Let's work on something — what have you done this week? Debussy?"

He pulled his chair over, already flipping pages, feeling around on the music rack for his pencil. "The Arabesque, good. Let's hear this, eh? How's it coming?" She said shyly, "All right," and bit her lip to keep from smiling as he found the pencil — discovered, for the third week in a row, that it was too blunt to write with — and absently stuck his hand inside the piano in the vague hope of retrieving another. Finding nothing, he settled back in his chair and took a large bite of toast and jam, glancing sideways at her. "You don't mind, eh? I haven't eaten yet today." He motioned towards the plate with his head. "Have a piece — go ahead. Are you hungry?" She shook her head. But the desire to laugh grew inside her — not that she wanted to laugh at *him* — it was just something about the whole way that he was, and what it was like being here, having her piano lesson, on a rainy Saturday afternoon and him eating toast with strawberry jam. It was always this way, here with him, and sometimes it made her laugh out loud, and he would glance at her, puzzled and surprised, and say, "I'm serious, Norma!" and she would have to say, "Yes, I know," and fight to keep her face straight, though the corners of her mouth still quivered.

He said, "So let's hear it," and she played through the Debussy, but it wasn't right, it was timid, opaque somehow, the tone was thin. She faltered, wanting to begin again, but he said sharply, "Continue!" and she kept on. At the end they both spoke at once:

"That wasn't any good — "

"You've got to learn to keep going."

She became quiet. His voice was now the voice she had heard while waiting in the hall; the shadow of his hand was very black against the printed page of music in front of her. "Here, at the beginning, you want to bring out these notes in the treble — almost a counter-melody — leading up to the high A. To the repetition of the high A," and again he picked up the blunt pencil, and tried vainly to circle the series of notes. "Damn pencil," he said, but for her the circles were there, bold and indelible.

"You know what I mean?"

She said quietly, "Yes, it's a kind of urgency, isn't it?" and he shot her an approving, almost grateful look: "Exactly, that's it. Urgency," as though that made the pencil-marks unnecessary. They worked the passage through.

The next time she played, it was closer to what she felt in this music — not just dreaminess, but a tingling sense of something about to happen . . . it's early spring . . . there's a stream, ice in it . . . small trees all around . . . there are still patches of snow on the ground. But everything is breaking up, melting . . . And through the melting, the shimmer of air, the shining water, she can still hear his voice, grave and quiet, saying, "Now lean into it. Move! Move with it! . . . Beautiful. Hear it? Can you feel the difference?"

Behind them, in the hall, the door opened twice: admitting the next student; admitting Mrs. Schwartz, slow-moving and silent, laden with grocery bags. On top of the piano his coffee, forgotten, got cold.

They went over all of it again. This time an electric current seemed to flow from the keys up through her fingers and all through her body. Her hands, lightly catching each other's phrases, seemed to ride on water: the clear, running notes were like water poured from hand to hand.

He was pleased. As she played, he kept casting her sidelong triumphant glances, eager to get her reaction. They smiled at each other; they laughed together. "You see? That's it, now. You've really got it."

Then he was saying ". . . late, Christ, I'm going to have to knock off . . ." and suddenly his voice changed, became sober and personal, and he asked quickly, in an undertone, "Listen, kid, how's the home situation these days?"

"It's all right," she said, not looking at him. But he must have caught something in her voice, for he persisted, "I mean, can you work?"

"Yes, when he's not home. I practice when he's not home." She felt, suddenly, close to tears, and wished he had not asked. He was shaking his head, muttering something — ". . . untenable situation . . . a shame . . ."

"It's really all right," she said huskily, barely above a whisper, and she cleared her throat and said it again, almost a plea — "It's really all right."

She ran the whole three blocks to the bus stop because she felt like running, and then stood still, listening to the pounding of her heart. Rain fell softly, misting the edges of things . . . Around her the streetlamps suddenly bloomed gold all up and down the street. For the moment it did not even matter that she was going home — to her mother playing Solitaire under the hairdryer, blowing on newly lacquered nails — to her father pacing up and down, reciting figures over the extension phone — to her brother standing at the window picking his nose. It didn't matter . . . In the bus she got a window seat, the only one left (surely a sign), and she sat with her cheek pressed to the cold glass, watching the magical streets rush past in a blur. Feeling she must shout aloud for the joy she held inside her:

(The black shingle roofs are shining under the lamps, under the rain; the sky darkens above the trees; wind bends the bare branches. This rain, now — will it be the last rain of the season? The birds are gone — the leaves have all come down — Now lights are going on in upstairs windows.)

A Nice Gazebo

I HAD A FRIEND who used to like walking by tennis courts in the city, late summer evenings. He wasn't a tennis player or wasn't interested in tennis, it wasn't like that. What he said he liked was the lighting. He liked how the courts looked, lit up at night; the burnish, almost pink, of those great lights, the pinkish radiance they put over things. How they made a separate world of the courts, the way stage lights do. They made it a different night there.

I had a friend. I say 'had' from a sense of past, of a time that is ended, though I believe we are still friends, we think of each other as friends. Only we do not see each other any more. We don't write, we don't phone; we live our lives separately in the same city, often, it may be, passing over the same ground, but at different times. We do, if we meet a mutual acquaintance, ask after each other. We would, if our paths crossed, stop to talk. (They have. We have.)

How it came to be this way is something too vague or stupid for me to explain, even to myself. I used to try, but it has been a long time since I've thought of it as something that needed explaining. Things are as they are, now, and I'm content to leave them this way. After a long interval of mulling and brooding, of measuring the time between visits, of lost sleep and shredded letters — at last I have no wishes, no predictions. I had a friend.

Moody chords on the piano. Low lighting. Shirts of dark plaid. Thick bean soups. What remains, of those we have cared for too much? "I like him, I like his face," someone said to me once, "he has eyes like a tavern door." And to my questioning laugh, "I don't mean the kind of tavern where men go to drink and brawl. I mean the kind they have in Ireland, that are family-run, they're private. The panes are frosted and you can see a light shining through at night, but you can't go in." Even when we were still seeing each other, I seldom dreamed about my friend, but when I did dream about him it was always the same: I broke something that belonged to him. Not on purpose, but I was still at fault. I picked up, I absently toyed with, something of his, and I was not careful. It came apart in my hands, or it fell and broke.

You see, I was at fault. I shouldn't have . . . I overstepped . . . I tried to go where it was not for me . . . But I wasn't going to talk about that.

It's grey today, and misty. Close, misty days of autumn rain, following one on another, without surprises. Just now I heard, across the street, a woman screaming at her child so terribly, it hurt me, it squeezed my heart. I got up and went over to the window to look: she was like a witch, in the doorway opposite, screaming. A woman my age, baby in arms, long hair caught back with a barrette. "How *dare* you! How *dare* you! And you'll come inside *right now*! Yes you *will*! And bring me my bag." The door slamming behind her.

And the child's heartbroken, bewildered wailing as he went back to do her bidding; the little fingers struggling to untie a knotted plastic shopping-bag from the handles of the smaller child's stroller . . . and still sobbing, to carry it, heavy, banging against his legs, inside to the monster mother.

I wanted to hurl myself out of the window and rescue him, I felt I could have killed her. But I know how great a measure of the hurt was that I saw myself, there. It was the witch in *me* that I wanted to kill. It was my own children I was hurting for, the ones I have screamed at, the ones I have dragged to do my bidding.

Another's child always cries more terribly than ours. We are inured to our own child's crying. We hear ordinary pain, in the other child's crying, but in our own child's, we hear only unusual pain. When our own child cries of ordinary pain, we say He's all right — he'll stop soon — it's not serious.

He always cries that way, we say blandly, apologetically, to the stranger on the sidewalk who stops in consternation. Don't worry, he's o.k., we say. It's not serious.

Sometimes my friend used to tell me his dreams, and sometimes I told him mine. This was years ago and I have forgotten the details, I don't remember particular dreams. But I remember that both of us dreamed recurringly of houses. In my friend's house dreams, the house was always the same, it was not a house he knew in real life, but in the dreams it was always familiar. It was a large house, classy, but comfortable too. He was in the house, he lived there, but apparently it did not belong to him completely. People would appear in it, unexpectedly, people he didn't know, partying, making themselves at home. Their sudden appearance, or his sudden awareness of their presence, frightened and disturbed him.

In my own house dreams, the houses were never the same, they were different houses every time, but they did belong to me. I had always just signed a lease, I was about to take up occupancy. In my dreams, I would be walking through the rooms, noticing defects I had overlooked, wondering how I could compensate for them. It was too late to change my mind, I was committed. The house was mine, whether I liked it or not. I was going to have to live there.

Sometimes I hear, second hand, a story that will stay with me all my life. Once a school girlfriend of mine, who had moved away to attend a different school, described to me how a boy in her class — an odd, shy boy, without friends, a misfit, universally made fun of — had sat at the lunch table next to hers in the cafeteria, and had taken from his crumpled paper bag a beautiful golden pear, a perfect pear, polished till it seemed to glow. "I don't know why it made me feel like crying," she told me. "I guess — it was realizing that he has a mother. He has a mother who loves him and chose that pear for him and washed it and shined it up specially and put it in his lunch. And she doesn't know. She doesn't know he's a creep. He's her little boy and she gave him a beautiful golden pear for his lunch. I can't explain.

Do you know what I mean?" I did; yes. "And he didn't even eat it."

My children, also, don't eat the pears I put in their lunches. The pears come back, two of them came home just yesterday, untouched, gone slightly mushy during the day, their skins blackened in patches, unappetizing. I washed the slime off them and cut away the soft parts and put them back in the refrigerator, and we had them sliced in our cereal this morning. "Don't give me pears in my lunch," my daughter said, perfunctorily. "Or bananas either. I *told* you — they turn yucky. How come you keep giving me them?"

I said, "I keep forgetting."

Would I know, if they were creeps?

When I scream at them, do they say to themselves, "It's o.k. — she'll stop soon — it's not serious"?

The last time I saw my friend, on the street, he was unshaven, perhaps he was beginning to grow a beard again. He had a beard when I first met him, but we weren't friends then, I was even a little afraid of him. He seemed suave to me, urbane in a way that I don't like; he seemed to me to be laughing at people. Then one day the beard came off and I saw him differently. I saw a shy chin that was not the chin I had imagined; I saw a boyish, gentle face. Soon after, we became friends. As I came to know him better, it was hard to imagine I had ever seen him the old way. Even when, from time to time, he grew the beard again, I couldn't see the person I'd been afraid of. But it was true I didn't like him as well with the beard, he seemed changed at those times. He became more aloof, more formal; he seemed withdrawn. And whenever he shaved it off — I sensed a return, a renewal of openness. I was always inclined to say, "Welcome back." Back from the Land of Beard.

I think that men grow beards to hide behind, at least in cultures where beards are a matter of choice. Maybe even where they're not. The Hasidic men I pass on the street are stern and remote behind their beards, safe from scrutiny in their resemblance to one another. My grandmother's father, in the portrait on her bureau, always struck my childhood eyes as a figure of awe. One cannot mistake the bearded man for a boy, nor easily see the boy in him. Of the men I've known who have grown beards and kept them, I'd say they were those most afraid of letting the boy show — those who had the highest stakes in hiding the boy, because the boy was too close to the surface. My husband has never worn a beard. But the boy is far, far away, in him.

And the girl in me? Not far, I think. I can call her back, can call back many stages of her growing, now for a moment I call back the age of nine, the age my son is now; she is in grade four, she has just changed schools because her family is moving, but for now they are all staying at her grandmother's, in the old neighbourhood, because the new house isn't ready. I see her let off by the school in the morning, one of the first in the schoolyard because her father, who drives her, starts work so early; I see how she lingers by the large painted "8" on the asphalt, the number of her classroom, where her class is to line up when the bell rings. She is a little diffident, she has not made friends here yet. She's a tall kid, her hair falls to her shoulders, straight and stringy, her breasts have not yet begun to bud, though in a few months that will all begin, the sudden tenderness around the nipples that will make it agony for her to be jostled in line or to bump against doorframes; in a few months, too, she will learn that she needs glasses, now she does not yet wear them, she does not have to feel in her pocket every few minutes to make sure the precious case is still there.

Every day this kid saves the fruit from her bagged lunch to eat on the school-bus going home. She is the only kid who stays for lunch — living too far, right now, to walk home — and she hates it. She hates the silence of the big empty classroom, the creeping movement of the red second-hand on the huge clock at the back of the room, the way the janitor comes in and pushes the broom up and down the empty rows and around her desk when she lifts her feet for him. After he goes out, she eats her sandwiches, chewing the dry bread with peanut butter and swallowing over and over, saving the milk from her thermos, trying to make it last the whole sandwich. She wads up the sticky waxed paper and throws it in the waste basket and then she sits at her desk and waits for the lunch hour to be over, waits out the silent eternity of it. The fruit, the pair of blue plums it has been, day after day, through this rainy autumn, she puts back in the brown paper bag with her thermos. It just fits in her desk, in the space between the two piles of text books, beside the wooden pencil-box that her mother bought her.

All the other girls have pink or blue vinyl pencil cases with zippers, embossed with hearts and flowers, or pony-tailed girls in slacks and poodles standing on their hind legs. She has mentioned this to her mother, but had demurred on the offer of one for herself. The inside of her desk is perfectly tidy, the larger books underneath, the smaller ones on top, the exercise books all together at the bottom on the left hand side, under her geography book. Sometimes there are other things in the desk, like the small stone shaped exactly like a potato, eyes and all, that she found by the fence in the schoolyard. It is a talisman, or a sort of pet; she takes it out with her at recess and holds it in her pocket, warms it in her fist inside her pocket, no one knows she has it. It's a magic potato, it sustains her without being consumed.

At three fifteen, when the bell rings, she gathers her books into the red satchel, fits the thermos in, and slips the bag of plums into her coat pocket. The yellow Uncle Harry wagon is always waiting outside, the sharp-faced French woman who drives it slouching back with her feet up, smoking a cigarette. The kid gets in and sits down on one of the hard benches that run the length of the van. The only other passengers, two French girls from another school, regard her without interest. As they lurch off, she takes the plums from her pocket and eats them. They are soft, deep blue with a silvery sheen. The insides are orangy-green and sweet, but the underside of the skin has a sour taste. After she has eaten the second one, the kid sucks on the stone until it has come perfectly clean, ridged and bone-hard. She keeps it in her mouth all the way home, for comfort, or maybe so she won't have to talk to the two French girls, not that they ever talk to her, nor would she be able to reply if they did, since she does not speak French. In school her class recites, dutifully, "La série," in various persons and tenses: *Je me lève, je vais à la fenêtre, j'ouvre la fenêtre, je ferme la fenêtre, je retourne à ma place, je m'assieds* — but she knows, somehow, reciting it to herself now, that this would not impress them. Having the stone to suck on gives her the courage of her own silence, and it helps to keep her from getting carsick as the school-bus lurches around corners, up and down the rainy Montreal streets, until it lets her off in front of her grandmother's apartment building. Relieved, faintly nauseated, she runs up the stairs . . . halls smelling of cooked cabbage . . . the paper bag with two plum stones crumpled in her hand.

My son speaks fluent French, carries a lunch box, forgets it often. Leaves it in school over the winter break, so the thermos comes back reeking so horribly of sour milk that we have to replace it. On his account we are called in to talk to the vice-principal and the school social worker; he has organization problems, they tell us, he loses homework, doesn't seem to be able to keep his desk in order. I fish my memory for solutions, explanations; I call the kid that I was onto the carpet and ask her sternly, "How did you learn to keep such a tidy desk? Why did you never lose your glasses?" But she looks at me in astonishment, it's nothing she does on purpose.

"When I was your age," we say to our children, as though it meant anything, as though it could help them. We try, absurdly, to use our past to map their future; "Go this way, that's how I went," we want to say, or "Don't go that way, that's where I fell," but we don't recognize that the actor is new, that the scenery has changed . . . My son cannot have been more than four when he said to his father, in response to some admonition or other, "Daddy, you do what *you* have to do — and I do what *I* have to do." A logic his father is fond of quoting.

We do what we have to do. It has a different ring to me, now, this statement, a more sombre one; more and more, it sounds like my life. Whole hours on automatic pilot. Moments when impatience overwhelms me, when I want to put the day on Fast Forward. Days of errands. Bank, groceries, pharmacy, post office. Slips of paper with lists on them, on my desk, in my handbag, in my pocket — they turn up everywhere. Kids to dentist. Buy bus passes. Get locks for bikes. Do taxes.

My friend, also, was a maker of lists, a writer of notes to himself. "Lately I find," I can hear him saying, it was an opener of his, "lately I find that if by the end of a day I've succeeded in doing the things I had to do, calmly and to the best of my ability, it's enough for me, I'm happy." We were talking about getting older, about diminishing expectations, about "happiness." I think it was an ongoing theme, with him, the idea of being happy with less. The idea that this is to be desired. Once he wrote me a long letter on the subject, a letter only partially tongue-in-cheek, in which he described (at what would have been excruciating length, coming from anybody else) the lunch that he packed for himself before setting out to work. The thermos full of hot soup made with beans, split peas, potatoes, onions, celery seed, dill seed, and parsley; the thick slices of rye bread, generously buttered; the raw carrots sealed in a plastic bag to keep them crisp. He described how he laid out this repast for himself, on a cardboard carton in the basement stockroom of the store where he worked, and how he ate it there, all by himself, away from the uproar of the shopping mall and office complex above.

"It's a kind of temple I make for myself," he wrote, and, "the carrots are so juicy, I don't even buy milk any more." At the end he wrote, "When I'm walking down the street with my knapsack full of good food, I have everything I want, I'm happy. I don't even need money then." What did I do with that letter? I think it was his credo. One ought not to misplace a person's credo.

"But is it really enough?" I asked him once, "I mean, don't you want the moon? I want the moon." And his low laugh, "Well, *sure*. Sure I want the moon. That's what the moon is for . . . only — " and the shift in tone to droll, confidential, "*the moon isn't interested in a wimp.*"

Grade Four, my children's school. They have called me in to do a little teaching, a special program. I want to read poems to the children, real poems, not the frisky whisky squirrel kind of poems I've seen posted in the corridors, copied neatly off the board in all their different handwritings and illustrated in Magic Marker.

But when I hand out my xeroxes of Theodore Roethke, of Emily Dickinson, and begin to read aloud, they aren't able to listen. Hands dart in the air, hands wave the sheet of paper at me. "Where do we put this?" they want to know. "Where does it go in our Poetry Binder? Do we put this into the Nature section? Do we put it with Nature or with People?" They are very worried about this. They have been made into bureaucrats by the age of nine. I'm reading them a poem, but before they can listen, they have to know what to file it under.

I feel bad for them. I feel bad for me. Be disorganized, I want to tell my son, it's okay.

A short history of my day: *Je me lève. Je vais à la fenêtre. J'ouvre la fenêtre. Je ferme la fenêtre. Je retourne à ma place. Je m'assieds.*

What else is there? *I get up*, the declaration of my active involvement in life. *I go to the window*, the assertion of my curiosity. *I open the window*: my statement of receptivity. (I open myself to what is out there. I air myself in it.) *I close the window*, the reassertion of my private self, retirement into solitude. *I return to my seat*, retreat to spiritual centre. *I sit down*, subside, that is to say, repose.

We recited this in all the persons, in all the tenses. *Tu te lèveras. Tu iras à la fenêtre. Tu ouvreras la fenêtre* . . .

It was tedious in the extreme.

He had two categories — my friend did — for talking about particulars in his life; things were 'boring' or they were 'thrilling.' The applications often surprised me. Boring for the botanical gardens, for modern dance, for tobogganing on the mountain. Thrilling for a woman's red shoes, for a large empty room with a polished floor, for big parties in bars. I don't know whether it was the polarization, or something else, that gave those words power to sting me: 'boring' like a slap in the face, 'thrilling' the amused put-down of an older brother. Was I juvenile, not to be bored? A sophomore, not to know enough to be thrilled? What an indictment they were, somehow, coming unexpectedly in the course of talk. Always they stopped me: have I missed something? He had a stance; almost, I envied it, but a little angrily.

I cannot think that he would have found the gazebo thrilling, though I think he should have. Gazebo, a word that I like, like 'cupola,' a word seen in print but never heard, so I don't even know how to pronounce it. Gazebo, a graceful word, part gazelle and part zebra, with the "o" at the end for a Spanish flavour. I suppose most people would call the little stage on the upper part of Fletcher's Field a bandstand. Rotunda — there's another of those words. But I prefer gazebo. I have always called it gazebo.

The gazebo on Fletcher's Field, by the fire station. Something gives it presence. Only once in ten years have I seen it used for anything formal, a band concert on a Sunday afternoon. "March from The Love of Three Oranges." Chabrier, "Espagnole." But children use it, and vagrants, and strolling friends and lovers, and clowning adolescents, these, wandering over the mountain, climb onto it almost absent-mindedly and make it their stage for a moment. Even when nobody is using it, it has a presence. Dreamy, it waits there on the green for the next comer, self-contained, carousel-like with its red and white paint, all ready for the players. It invites you to come up and act out your moment. I like to see it there, waiting, especially in the early morning as my bus rolls over the mountain towards the Métro. To see it emerging dimly from November fog rose-lit by the first rays of sun; to see it bright and candy-coloured under a Wedgwood sky, against a field of snow; or cheerful after winter against the greys and browns of uncovered ground. It has almost a human presence. The presence is that of a small girl playing alone, a girl with a crown of braids, singing to herself. Gazebo.

For a long time I never thought about the gazebo, never noticed myself noticing it. How it came into my thoughts was that one night, about three years ago, I dreamed it was gone.

At that time I had not been remembering my dreams. I had not been thinking about dreams or dreaming. But I met a woman who was in Jungian analysis, who lived vividly with her dreams and told them in technicolour, church pageant dreams, full of priests and violins. I said to her, "I never remember my dreams any more, I wonder if I dream at all?" and as I spoke, I remembered dreaming about the gazebo the night before.

I was on the bus, rolling over the mountain towards the Metro as usual, and as we approached the fire station I noticed the gazebo was gone. And I thought to myself, "Oh yes, that's right, it burned down." I thought I remembered someone telling me it had burnt down. And I thought, "What a shame for the children!"

That was all there was to it, my gazebo dream, but in the remembering of it I was so struck by its realism that I thought it might be true that the gazebo had burnt down. *Hadn't* somebody mentioned that to me, in passing? And I had felt a sharp, fleeting regret, and then forgotten about it. Yes, the conversation had moved to other things and I hadn't had the chance to return to it, absorb it. It got buried.

But could that be true, then, that the gazebo was gone? But why the sharp regret? Had I ever been aware that the gazebo meant something to me? No, I had never thought about it one way or another. It was only a landmark, a familiar one, passed by almost daily, taken for granted. Yes, sometimes the children liked to climb on it and play, when we walked over the mountain. But not so as to notice — except maybe months later, a startled moment in passing — that it was gone. Not so as to notice they missed it.

It would go as so many things went, the elms along Sherbrooke Street, whole rows of run-down shops, certain old buildings endowed with lesser historic interest. It would go without fanfare, and the city would not rebuild it. Studies would show it had not been much used, it served no purpose. People would soon forget it had ever been there, if they noticed its absence at all.

So I gloomed, in a civic huff. Another loss. Another impoverishment. Another reason to shake my fist at City Hall. But then, maybe a day later, riding the bus downtown,

I looked out across the green to confirm this latest outrage, and there was the gazebo, intact.

So it wasn't true! So I *had* only dreamed it! Relief flooded me, inexplicable gratitude; it was still there. I felt as if I had narrowly escaped something. I felt as one feels when, after digging through all the compartments of one's handbag in a rising panic, one reaches into one's coat pocket and finds the wallet there.

Later I pondered: why all this about the gazebo? Why the fuss? And I wondered what my dream had meant. In the dream, I did not consider my own loss, but thought, "What a shame for the children." I wrote the dream down in my daybook, but it wasn't until recently, coming across the entry, that its meaning became apparent. There on the page opposite, the same day or the day before, was an entry complaining that life seemed to have lost its liveliness and colour, that I felt closed up, untouched by things. It's so clear to me now, what the gazebo of my dream represented: the arena for the creative, for imagination, playfulness, delight; the little theatre of inner life. I had that dream at a time when it was as though my own gazebo had burnt down — a time when I had not been remembering my dreams, when I had not been thinking about dreams or dreaming. It is "a shame for the children" when adults lose their gazebo. When I think of the dream now, I think that "What a shame for the children" didn't mean only my children, but the whole idea of children, of generation, in a culture. We need a culture that rebuilds its gazebo, keeps it in good repair. A culture that guards the gazebo for its children.

That's what it was about my friend. He had a nice gazebo. He had a way of making play, of rearranging things. He could cut snippets of print out of magazines, half a sentence here, three words there, and tape them onto the pages of a pocket notebook to make a zany little book, enigmatic, witty, and whimsical, for an evening's delight, to show and share. And he could find the little book stuck inside a real book, three years later, only to discover that the scotch tape had lost its stick and the words were floating loose between the pages; and instead of sticking them back in place, he could flip them over and be fascinated by the bits of coloured, glossy picture-fragments on the reverse, tags and shreds of magazine images long gone. He could dispense with the little book forthwith and take those strips of paper, turned on their coloured sides, fasten them with pearl-studded straight pins onto a cork board, call it "my butterfly collection," and be delighted all over again. A kind of recycling, a fluid art. On top of a stereo speaker in his living-room he had, for the longest time, a curious arrangement of objects: a slab of black slate, upon which stood an empty wineglass, grown dusty, and a glass pill vial containing an iridescent green beetle. "History Lesson #5: The Ice Age" was typed on a piece of paper taped to the speaker. First, my friend explained to me, the wineglass had been filled with ice cubes. They melted. Then the water evaporated. Now the glass was filmed in dust. It had taken a while. He found that thrilling.

My friend's gazebo. The way he'd move his furniture around, his bed from room to room. How he'd pillage the alley, drag in old wooden sofa frames and fit them up with dusty cushions. How he'd collect dead televisions. In the spring, everything went back out to the alley. "I've had enough," he'd say.

Those were days when I visited often, dropping in for coffee in the course of a day's errands if I knew it was his day off, manoeuvring my daughter's stroller up the leaning stairs if I had her with me, as usually I did. He'd serve me lunch sometimes: an enormous bowl of steamed vegetables, potatoes and carrots and cauliflower and turnips and broccoli, well buttered with salt and pepper. A simple meal, yet somehow celebratory, a feast. He'd tell me about something he'd heard on the radio, an amusing story, an odd news item. Or he'd tell me an anecdote about somebody who'd come into the store that week. I'd tell him what my son had said at the breakfast table. Sometimes he lent me books that I would take home and read as if for clues to who he was. If I found underlinings, marginal notations, I could ponder them for days. I rarely found any, and when I did, they were gnomic. Anyhow, he bought most of his books second-hand, so how could I even be sure they were his markings?

And he, too, visited often, delighting the children with ambushes from behind easy chairs, tackle and tumble games; sharing a 6-pack with their father, talking politics, talking new movies. That was whose friend he was to begin with, their father's; and very quickly he became their friend, and only gradually, mine. I would always have to excuse myself early on, to see to putting the children to bed, reading or singing to them in the big upholstered rocker. I don't know why I was sure he was listening to me singing, even while I could hear their conversation going on in the kitchen, above the clatter of dishes as my husband cleared table from dinner. If I sang beautifully enough, if I wove a spell with my singing, I could keep him there, he would not leave before the children fell asleep and I could join them again for a late cup of tea. At the beginning he sometimes left before; he'd tip-toe past the living-room door, put his head in for just a second and raise a hand at me by way of good night. Later he inevitably stayed till I was free. Sometimes he stayed very late.

I don't have to say what happened. Nothing happened. That's what's embarrassing, I guess, that nothing happened, that something could have happened but didn't, that things almost happened but in the end, nothing was even spoken aloud, nothing was acted out or mutually imagined. There were some moments, a summer evening on the roof, an October afternoon on some swings in the park, there was some giddiness, some reckless gaiety, that was all. Was that all? No, there were a couple of quarrels, lightning-like, coming out of nowhere and leaving a rawness, bewilderment, in their wake. And then the spacing of visits. Mine, his. He found a girlfriend. He moved.

Nous avons fermé la fenêtre. Nous avons retourné à nos places. Nous nous sommes assis.

He stopped coming around. You see, it was that simple. He stopped, not abruptly, but little by little, like a weaning. One didn't have to notice. At our age, people got busy, people's lives changed, friends drifted. No explanation was called for, on either side. By that time in my life, friendships of far more substance had dwindled to an exchange of letters around Christmas, an occasional long-distance call, or, even with people who'd not left town, an annual, ritual dinner. There was no call for surprise. Yet in his case, for a long time, I blamed myself. I'd asked too much of him. I hadn't asked enough.

I was seventeen when I worked my first real job, one of a number of civil-service summer positions created especially for students. My parents, who had recently moved to Ottawa, helped me to find it. I was assigned to the Crustal Geology Division of the Department of Energy, Mines, and Resources, where I sat behind a frosted glass partition in a small suite on the sixteenth floor of a concrete office tower, and typed geologists' field reports. I do not remember very much about the job, whether it was only field reports that I typed, or whether I also typed other things, perhaps less interesting. Of the field reports I remember words like mica schist, bore-hole, granoblastic, a bleb of charnokite; these kept me going, more or less. What I chiefly remember is the shock of finding out that there was no use at all in trying to work faster in order to "get finished" what they'd given me, that getting a pile of typing done didn't mean I was then free to think my own thoughts, gaze out the window, read a book in my lap, or type a letter to a friend ("Here I am on the sixteenth floor of a white concrete office building, typing field reports for geologists . . .") No, if I was quick to finish a pile of typing, I would be given another pile of typing, and another and another until lunchtime, and after that, the same again until five. It was the beginning of "doing what we have to do" for me, as school had never been, and I didn't like it.

That was an exceptionally hot summer. I remember standing at the bus stop in the blazing sun at five o'clock, my nylons sticking, feeling the heat radiate up from the pavement that seemed to be made of shimmering, splintered light; I remember looking at the bus-stop crowds, the men and women in business suits streaming out of concrete towers identical to mine, on both sides of the street, and thinking, *This is what they do, every day. Not just for the summer. This is their life.*

There must have been other students assigned to departments in my building, but I never met any, and I was the only one in my division. So even at lunch hour, there was no one to talk to, no real diversion. Yet my lunch hours are what I remember most clearly, remember fondly, even wistfully, at odd moments. I brought my lunch from home (packed for me, indulgently, by my mother, who was pleased to have me home from college and working in town for the summer). The office complex happened to be only a couple of blocks from the river, where bicycle paths and walkways defined a wide swath of green parkland. Here I headed at twelve thirty with my brown paper bag and book, the book I had chosen to read that summer, for reasons only my seventeen-year-old self (were I to call her back) could explain to you. The book was *The Socratic Dialogues of Plato*, not exactly light summer reading. I made a place for myself on the grass in the shade of a cluster of split, aging black willows, and there, in the breeze off the river, by the glinting water, I ate my lunch and read Plato. I had elected, for the following year, to major in philosophy; this was my entrée.

My mother packed wonderful lunches. Usually I had a sandwich of cream cheese on black bread, garnished with pimento olives. Sometimes, if she had baked that week, there was a large piece of homemade cake wrapped in layers of foil and waxed paper, slightly misshapen, thickly iced, with gobs of frosting clinging to the waxed paper for me to lick off, absently, while the civilized, gentle voices of dead Greeks rose to me from the pages of my book. What I saved for last was the little packet of foil-wrapped almonds and raisins, and my apple. Oh, wonderful apple! Day after day, a giant glowing-green Granny Smith apple, heavy with juice, perfectly balanced between tart and sweet. An apple to take the fur off one's teeth, a green dream of an apple.

Various people had warned me that majoring in philosophy wouldn't be much like sitting in my room and thinking. I lasted two years as a philosophy major, bewildered by the aridity of semantics, the necessity for secondary sources. Nothing I studied in those two years had the magic of Plato under those trees by the river, where seagulls walked around me on the grass, picking up sandwich crusts, and the discourse of Socrates, punctuated by soothing "Assuredly's," "Most certainly's," "It would seem so's" from his disciples, came inextricably entwined with the breezy green sweetness of my Granny Smith apple. Of my fellow students, only one stood out, a tall, stunning young woman who, at a time when 'natural' was the watchword, came to class wearing brilliant red lipstick, dyed her hair platinum blond, dressed with a shocking, flamboyant individuality. I never was able to follow a thing she said in class, but she had a reputation for being brilliant, if a little crazy, and she outlasted me by many years in the philosophy department. I mention this woman, Frieda, only because she turned up later in another guise, she was one of the mothers in a cooperative playgroup my children attended when they were small; she had a daughter my son's age. Once, at a playgroup meeting (these were frequent and tedious), the primary teacher brought up the question of whether we thought the children were old enough to handle play dough. Frieda, who had been slumped in a semi-stupor across the table from me, woke up, startled. "Plato?" she said wonderingly. "*Plato*? I think they're *much* too young." This is the sort of thing I used to like to share with my friend, in those days.

Playgroup operated mornings only; each week day, a different mother came in to assist the teacher, and provided a cooked lunch for the children. We had this coordinated for variety; you brought the same lunch each time your turn came up; everyone brought something different. I was bean stew. Everyone was also expected to contribute to the play value of the group by sharing some area of expertise; reading a special-interest story, leading an activity. Frieda, the philosopher, who at this point in her life taught aerobics, was supposed to do exercises with them. Other mothers did other things. Once, dubious as to how much was really happening in this regard (probably because my own attempts at keeping the attention of nine pre-schoolers were so often abortive) I tried to quiz my son about the others.

"Do you like it when Janet comes?" I asked him. Janet was the organic gardener. "Is it fun for you when Janet is a teacher?"

"Ya," he said right away. "I like the macaroni when she comes." So I tried again. "How about Frieda? Do you have fun when Frieda comes?"

This took a longer time, but not much. "I don't like the bananas part of the cottage cheese."

This, too, I shared with my friend. It was the kind of thing he liked to hear, a little nugget out of an ordinary day, something quirkily funny, a bit subversive. I liked to watch him savour such an item: the second of absorbing it, considering the angles; then the quiet, the appreciative, laugh; the gentle, somehow almost rueful laugh; the laugh I'd store things up all week for the chance of drawing from him, the pleasure of that. For really there was a very great pleasure in it. "That's nice," he'd say, in his private, his happily intimate, voice, leaning a little on the word 'nice,' giving to it a special weight of significance, of pleased surprise, making it an accolade.

"That's *nice*," is what he'd say.